Little Nation
& Other Stories

ALEJANDRO MORALES

Translated from the Spanish by Adam Spires

Little Nation
& Other Stories

ALEJANDRO MORALES

Translated from the Spanish by Adam Spires

Arte Público Press
Houston, Texas

Little Nation and Other Stories is made possible through a grant from the City of Houston through the Houston Arts Alliance. We are grateful for their support.

Recovering the past, creating the future

Arte Público Press
University of Houston
4902 Gulf Fwy, Bldg 19, Rm 100
Houston, Texas 77204-2004

Cover design by Mora Des¡gn
Cover art by José Esquivel

Morales, Alejandro, 1944- author.
  [Novellas. Selections. English]
    Little nation and other stories / Alejandro Morales ; translated from the Spanish by Adam Spires ; with an introduction by Adam Spires.
      p. cm.
    ISBN 978-1-55885-801-5 (alk. paper)
  I. Spires, Adam, translator. II. Title.
PQ7079.2.M6A2 2014
863'.64—dc23

                                                              2014022867
                                                                     CIP

♾ The paper used in this publication meets the requirements of the American National Standard for Information Sciences—Permanence of Paper for Printed Library Materials, ANSI Z39.48-1984.

Printed in the United States of America

14 15 16 17 18 19 20   10 9 8 7 6 5 4 3 2 1

Contents

"Alejandro Morales: Writing Chicano Space"
by Adam Spires **vii**

Quetzali **1**

Mama Concha **11**

The Gardens of Versailles **27**

Prickles **43**

Little Nation **83**

Write the things which thou hast seen,
and the things which are,
and the things which shall be hereafter.

Revelation 1:19

Alejandro Morales:
Writing Chicano Space

As the title "Little Nation" implies, the short stories in this latest collection from Alejandro Morales underscore the significance of marginalized space and the political will to defend it. A Chicano national space within the United States is a point of contention that characterizes the greater part of the works of Alejandro Morales, a writer who has distinguished himself at home and abroad as one of the Chicano Movement's most renowned spokesmen, as evidenced by his worthy tribute: the Luis Leal Award for Distinction in Chicano/Latino Literature, 2008. In this collection of short stories, the word "nation" evokes the Chicano's history of unity, belonging and ancestral pride. Though reborn in the 1960s as "Aztlán"—the birthplace of the Aztecs, of Mexicans and of today's Chicanos, this is a nation that remains absent from any conventional map. Depending on one's perspective, Aztlán could easily be dismissed as a relic of mythology, rather than a geographical reality. And yet, there are these concentrations of proud people, united by their long history of civilization and by their collective effort to assert their claims, who have lived in Aztlán for centuries. Arguably, it is this heightened sense of belonging that exacerbates the Chicano's marginal status. Compared to the colossus that surrounds them, the Chicano nation is indeed little and, accordingly, its national concerns are of little consequence to the status quo. In *Little*

Nation and Other Stories, as in his earlier narratives, Morales once again combines the two opposing forces of national pride and marginalization to produce a representation of Chicano space beleaguered by conflict.

Through his literature Morales evinces an acute sense of space: specifically, how the space beneath one's feet relates to the space between one's ears, how Chicanos and Chicanas search for their roots in a space occupied by a hegemonic Other, how identity is destabilized when space is fractured by borders, and how the disparities between marginalized space and central powers upset the balance of society. This focus on spatial dynamics also lends itself to a more universal appeal, for our relationship to space, or *topos*, defines who we are, especially when this relationship is called into question. Under duress, our imagination tends to take one of two divergent paths. From a positive outlook, *u*topia is conjured up as an unattainable ideal. It is a space that we keep in our hearts, a space that inspires us to keep dreaming and, for some, to keep fighting. In contrast, *dys*topia is the ill-fated space of the future, a nightmare that haunts us should we continue along the injudicious path of complacency and allow ourselves to be erased from our native space. Examples of these two extremes are readily available in the works of Alejandro Morales, but there is yet another space, a middle ground that balances precariously between dream and nightmare that has proven to be of particular interest to the novelist. The multiple realities that surround Morales in Aztlán, where cultural disorder is the norm, are captured by his vision of *hetero*topia, a concept developed originally by the French theorist Michel Foucault in *The Order of Things*. Neither Mexico, nor the U.S., nor Aztlán *per se*, but rather, all at once, the American Southwest is a space marked by contrasts and struggles that create new mythologies and new identities, constructed from the fragments of endless cultural collision. Often the effort to normalize Latino difference amidst the ubiquitous influence of the Anglo leads to cracks in the armor of resistance. Thus it only stands to reason that in *hetero*topia identity is in constant need of repair. As Morales writes:

> Chicanos have become trapped in the process of self-definition and have splintered, shattered their identity, made themselves an ambiguity, strangers in their own land, constantly moving like migrants, not knowing who they are, where they come from, nor where they are going. They fail to understand that identity is not fixed, that nothing is certain in the Southwestern heterotopia border zone. (Morales 1996: 24)

Much has been written about the border and its relationship to identity, and Morales is no exception. The notorious space that divides the two nations figures prominently in his sensitivity to injustice and to fractured identities. As for Aztlán herself, Morales takes the position that heterotopia's mixture of cultural incongruities creates numerous internal borders as well. Life for the Chicano/a demands the continual process of navigating across borders, potentially destabilizing one's sense of wholeness. The writer's task, as dubious as it may be, is to somehow weigh a cultural mooring into this sea of ever shifting undercurrents to claim a recognizable space to call home. Ultimately what surfaces is a cause and effect relationship between the illusory sense of belonging in heterotopia, and a representation riled by the grim experience of marginalization. It is as if Morales were clearing the reader's head of a utopian dream turned dystopian nightmare with a wake-up call to the reality that Chicanos/as still have to elbow their way into society. As he concludes plainly, "this sense of being simultaneously 'inside' and 'outside' is a manifestation of the utopian desire to belong, which is unattainable in heterotopia" (Morales 1996: 25).

For over forty years, Morales has been articulating the complex relationship between space and identity through his academic writing, novels, poetry, and short stories, including this recent collection. He figures prominently as one of the most prolific of Chicano writers with works disseminated internationally through translation into multiple languages. He has also received much acclaim for the experimental nature of his works. While his literary contribution to the Chicano Movement remains unwavering, the structure and style of his writing are constantly evolving. It is this unique combination of infusing the local cause with artistic invention that Gurpegui identifies as Morales's trademark "double compromise" (2). Indeed Morales's creative process appears unrestricted by any conventional approach to writing. Akin to the stylistic of the *nouveau roman*, his works tend to evade a singular focus on plot and character development to allow for an array of images, voices and spaces which contribute to a portrayal of a daunting authenticity aptly conveyed through writing. Moreover, each literary project constitutes a departure in literary technique from the former, attesting to his drive toward innovation and, in true artistic fashion, to discover or create new forms of expression. As such, Morales has proven himself a veritable pioneer of a variety of narrative techniques, and he remains a standout for his daring posture.

Nowhere is this more evident than in his first novel, *Caras viejas y vino nuevo* (1975)[1], with which he unleashed a hardcore representation of Chicano reality in the barrio. Stemming from his own early days of destruction when he inhabited the barrio underworld, in *Caras*, poverty, violence, self-contempt and exclusion are the notable signifiers. Published in Mexico, the novel was a misfit in the greater scheme of the Chicano

---

[1]See *Barrio on the Edge* (1998) for the bilingual edition of *Caras*, translated by Francisco Lomelí.

Movement, which sought to bring about and celebrate a cultural revival. In hindsight, this would prove to be Alejandro's way, impelled by his uncompromising commitment to tell the disconcerting stories of those who suffer at the margin, in the space that society would rather forget. Reminiscent of the Latin American "boom" novel, *Caras* is highly experimental, unhindered by market expectations, one of the author's most celebrated works for its shrewd originality. Not surprisingly the representation of space in this novel is especially worthy of note. As Francisco Lomelí argues,

> [I]t was not enough to re-create an ambience in strictly realistic terms, a place that could be identified and located on a map. Instead, Morales chose a refraction of various barrios into one metaphorical barrio that is anonymous, geographically imprecise—although he indicates that it is in the general area of Los Angeles—and devoid of physical markers except for "this side" and "the other side." What concerns Morales is an experiential, subjective barrio—a state of being rather than a place—that questions referents and the activity of referents. People live here, experience it from within, and perpetuate its vices as well as its virtues. The barrio has a life of its own, much like a cultural entity that marches to its own rhythm and conflictive circumstances. (Lomelí 1998: 7)

Lomelí explains further that, written in a hyperrealistic mode, or, "mystic realism" (8), a hallucinated sense of space is fitting for a cast of characters who experience daily the mind-altering world of drugs, violence and depravity. Even the language itself is characterized by ellipses, gaps in speech and memory, and distortions of syntax, leaving much to the reader's imagination. In sum, Morales broke into the literary (crime) scene with arguably one of the most accurate and, without a doubt, one of the most creative reflections of the chaos of barrio life.

In his second novel, *La verdad sin voz* (1979), it is a forgotten story, though not an uncommon one, that Morales voices. Based on a Mathis, Texas, homicide from the 1970s, in *La verdad* Morales recounts the life and death of an Anglo doctor who devoted his life to migrant Mexican laborers in a space where poor Mexicans know their place and where the dominant Anglo society has no tolerance for dangerous agents of change. This is literature with a cause, specifically, to bring to light the excesses of violence and prejudice that characterize the local authority's oppression of the marginalized: a point made poignantly clear when the idealistic doctor is shot and killed by the local sheriff. As Gurpegui describes it, "the novel is a veritable battle field [. . .] denying any possibility of a happy ending" (Gurpegui 1996: 2). As in his first novel, Morales eludes the standard focus on a central protagonist, choosing instead to interweave three different story lines: the death of an Anglo, the adversities faced by a Latino professor and Mexico's troubles with modernization. And here we also see a precursor of Morales's historical writing—a genre that would thereafter hold his attention—whereby he combines his research skills with a flair for artistic reconfiguration to produce an alternative history of Aztlán.

This kind of corrective historiography, invigorated by compelling personal stories that convey an alternate view of the past, is consolidated in his three historical novels: *Reto en el paraíso* (1983), *The Brick People* (1988) and *River of Angels* (2014), where the question of space—land seizures, alienation and exclusion from the center—are again brought to the fore. Beginning with *Reto*, Morales chronicles the struggles of the nineteenth-century Californios whose prominence in society sharply declines as their space, passed down from generations, is inundated by the tide of westward expansion. Challenging the monopoly over the official story held by Anglo historians like Hubert Howe Bancroft and Leonard Pitt, Morales brings history's prominent Californios to life to supposedly speak for themselves, empowering them with a voice of their own and, more importantly, a will of resistance. Infused with meaningful corollaries that play themselves out in the future, *Reto* epitomizes the formula that characterizes much of Morales's novels, insofar as Chicano identity balances precariously between the woes of a precolonial utopia and a sense of urgency over an intensifying postcolonial dystopia. In this regard, there is no mistaking the causal relationship between the Gringo's "technology of death" (Morales 1983: 286) and a new "world of decadence" (286) devoid of the Mexican's ancestral values and traditions. Once again in defiance of market demands, Morales produced a text that challenged the public. A bilingual novel consisting of separate configurations in lieu of a chronological sequence of chapters, the narrative jumps between Spanish and English, the past and present, and between numerous main characters. Though there is no central protagonist, there is one character who deserves special attention here. Incapable of reconciling the contradictions between the alleged glorious history of the Californios and their obvious demise in an Anglo-dominant world, the pseudo-autobiographical "Dennis" fails to embrace the Chicano Movement.[2] As a result, Dennis, the "crazy split brain man" (278) is left to decay in a scene reminiscent of Kafka's *Metamorphosis*. Arguably at his best in the role of Devil's advocate, in *Reto*, Morales lays bare the uncomfortable reality that "it is impossible to recreate Aztlán in this modern world" (297).

---

[2]Unbeknownst to many of Morales' readers, the author's official name is Alexander Dennis Morales, whereas "Alejandro" is his pen name.

By comparison, the tone in *The Brick People* (1988) is noticeably more hopeful as he tells the story of Mexicans living in Simons, a segregated town on the outskirts of Montebello constructed by the Simons Brick Company at the turn of the twentieth century. Though a portrayal of marginalization does figure in the main, the saga does not revolve around a litany of injustices, but rather it consists of an unsung history of how Mexican labor was the driving force behind the building of California. It is a story of pride and of hope as factory work attracted Mexicans from as far away as Guanajuato and Michoacán, who braved the long journey in search of a better life. It is a chapter in California history that Morales knows well in a space that he holds dear to his heart, for *The Brick People* is inspired by the lives of his mother and father. Therein lies the cause whereas, in terms of literary technique, Antonio Márquez contends that, in *The Brick People* Morales adopts a narrative style more akin to postmodernism than to the traditional historical novel. Strategically it allows the novelist to instill his ( )story of Simons with more personal accounts of the abused Mexican workers. Márquez explains further that:

> The brick factory and the generations of workers form a collective metaphor in the golden land with eyes on the American dream. However, the individual is not subsumed to history. Morales's brand of 'intrahistory' valuates the individual and affirms moments of human struggle often forgotten in the wake of history. History must share the stage with myth, and Morales takes the avenue of magic realism to bring about that blend. (Márquez 1996: 80)

As in the case of *Reto*, the portrayal of the past is complemented in *The Brick People* by a retrospection into a dystopian future, evocative of Orwell's maxim that "he who controls the past, con-

trols the future." Thus the rise of modernization bodes ill for the
Mexican laborer who, tethered to the Machine, remains dependent on the Anglo's control over the economic means and the
technological modes of production. As one man concludes plainly to his fellow brick workers: "Electricity is a gringo plague that
will infect us and make us sick. They will make us like thousands
of stupefied moths attracted to and trapped by this pretty light
until we burn" (Morales 1988: 204). As explained further on, it is
the predicament of the marginalized in the ill-fated space of the
future that reduces the Mexican laborer even further down the
entomological scale, namely from the above-cited "stupefied
moths" to "Mexicans, like cockroaches" (126).

   In *River of Angels,* his most recent novel, Morales returns to
the early twentieth century to chronicle the lives of two families
brought together to build the first bridges across the
Porciúncula, the Los Angeles River. Mexicans were needed to
build the bridges, and bridges, ironically, were needed to get
Mexican laborers out of affluent Los Angeles and back to the
other side: "work for us here, but live, die and be buried over
there on the Eastside" (xii). It is the history of how an unpre-
dictable flowing border segregates the Mexican population
during the tenuous 1920s. The economic fallout of the Great
Depression coupled with the rise of Aryanism leads to the sys-
tematic targeting of Mexicans for scapegoating, racial
discrimination and deportation. But like the powerful river herself, the flow of Mexican migration within her homeland, the
heart of Aztlán, is a natural phenomenon, and not easily con-
tained. Departing from his customary depiction of fierce
resistance, in *River of Angels,* Morales mitigates conflict with a
seemingly boundless capacity for patience and understanding.
Another difference is the linear storyline, without the disrup-
tions in sequential narrative that we see in his earlier historical

novels. There is, nonetheless, no mistaking the recurring motifs that have become a hallmark of Alejandro Morales' body of works, symptomatic of his drive to honor the legacy of California's Mexican workforce. Here again we bear witness to the emerging captains of industry who shaped Los Angeles with Mexican laborers manning the front lines. The novel features strong female roles, challenging the prejudices of the day, and quasi mystical characters that unavoidably draw out society's intolerance of the unfamiliar. The love and respect that fortify Mexican family bonds are inspiring and, in consequence, they stir the righteous indignation of the reader when families are threatened by corrosive ideologies. Most notable are the protagonists who develop in proportion to their sense of space, to their ancestral relationship to the river and adjacent lands:

> He remembered his parents, he remembered when he was Otchoo Ríos and when he felt a part of the river, the land, felt he belonged here. [. . .] For generations his family had lived in Los Angeles. He and his family, more than anyone else, belonged here! He and his family were not aliens, not immigrants. This was their land. (152)

The Porciúncula may have receded to a trickle compared to the often raging waters of the past, but the longstanding cultural divide between its two shores remain anchored in place. What Morales reminds us in *River of Angels,* is that this division was not by chance, but rather, it was a separation of cultures by design.

Unique to his body of works is the novel, *The Rag Doll Plagues* (1992), which comprises three parallel stories set, respectively, in Mexico's colonial past, modern-day California, and during the reign of the Triple Alliance in the year 2027. The plot within each period is advanced by the returning motif of an epidemic:[3] first as *La Mona* (a disease similar to leprosy), then contemporized as AIDS, and, finally, as an ecological plague that defies the technology of the future. In each time-space, the suffering and decay of the sick and dying are portrayed in graphic detail, particularly among the poor, who are routinely abandoned by the Establishment. Culling a familiar premise from his earlier historical works, *Rag Doll* draws from the mistakes of the past to forecast a full-fledged dystopia in the future redolent of more canonical novels, such as Orwell's *Nineteen Eighty-Four* and Huxley's *Brave New World*. But Morales adds a startling twist, whereby the future Apocalypse befalls the upper class instead of the standard portrayal of suffering masses. Indeed, his bitter irony comes to light unambiguously in a representation of Mexico's beleaguered poor who, after centuries of living in the most unsanitary conditions imaginable, develop immunity to pestilence. When wealthy families come to depend on blood transfusions from Mexican migrants, it becomes clear that, in the future, only the details will change in the long history of Mexican subordination to the economic and, in this case, life-saving interests of the North. The trends in globalization that broaden a free-flow access to the Mexican commodity have marked Morales's worldview throughout his entire life and, accordingly, he has responded with an unsettling forewarning in this work of speculative fiction, the first of its kind in Chicano literature.

Morales' interest in spatial dynamics is clearly illustrated in his ongoing literary project subtitled "the heterotopian trilogy." In the first of these, *Waiting to Happen* (2001), the reader

---

[3]Facing these epidemics is the repeated role of a physician, "Gregorio," so named undoubtedly in honor of the author's son, Gregory, who is also a physician.

returns to the daunting space of the drug world, where the injustices of the cross-border relationship are aggravated further by government corruption and violent crime. It is a pressing reality that haunts both sides from an unmanageable no-man's-land. While a blunt representation of this austere space corrodes our reading with one horror story after the next, the impact is somewhat mitigated by sacred agents from the past who portend yet another Apocalypse. The protagonist "J.I." is the less-than-sublime prophet who defiles herself in effigy to Mexico's legacy of sin. Her bodyguard is the monster Endriago—"a grotesque but intelligent man" (Morales 2001: 92)—a Cyclops with clairvoyance, a veritable modern-day Quasimodo. But as the right-hand man of the brutal anti-narcotics brigade, Endriago mutates seamlessly into an arsonist, torturer, and murderer, living up to the meaning of his name, "monster devourer of virgins" (92). Indeed, if the dystopian motifs of earlier novels cast a shadow of misery over the future of Aztlán, in *Waiting to Happen*, Morales pollutes them further with an amplification of the abject suffering and debasement that take place behind dystopia's veil of modernity. And herein lies the crux of the matter. Analogous to Bernard McKelroy's contention that "in the modern grotesque, we are not invited to ask what power might change a man into an insect or a woman into a machine as some kind of cosmic joke. The attention, rather, is directed to the predicament of the besieged and humiliated self in its struggle with the brutal and brutalizing other" (McKelroy 1989: 184). Morales employs an array of grotesque imagery to convey the very real effects of marginalization, the brutality with which the modern world (read, First World economy) dehumanizes Mexico's most destitute. In effect, Morales does depict a woman transformed into a machine, "the artiorgans" (Morales 1983: 349), and men into insects, "the cockroach people" (Morales 1988: 126), to say nothing of the gruesome decay of the human body portrayed throughout *Rag Doll*. In so doing, he sheds light on Aztlán's cultural decay in an effort to imbue his readers with a sense of resentment on behalf of those who suffer Third World conditions within arm's reach of the American Dream. On this subject, I once asked Alejandro why he continues to intensify his dystopian outlook with such depictions of a grotesque world. He replied quite frankly that, on the contrary, "it is not a *grotesque* world. It is a very *real* world. I have seen all of that myself, either in Mexico or the United States" (Spires 2001: 266). This is his compromise. He writes the unspeakable for those without a voice, lost in the ever-widening gap between the rich and the poor in an increasingly dehumanized world.

In a similar manner, navigating through the familiar territory of poverty, disease and their political implications for Mexicans in the U.S., in *The Captain of All These Men of Death* (2008) Morales combines a personal story with a genealogy of tuberculosis, yet another plague that has shaped social behavior for millennia. Based in large part on the testimonials provided by Alejandro's uncle, Roberto Contreras (an ex-TBer), and on research conducted by Alejandro's son, Gregory (who wrote a case study on the disease), this novel also weaves in an extensive historical account of the world's continued effort to cure TB. From Hippocrates to Montezuma, from La Llorona to Frankenstein, from Auschwitz to Simons, Morales takes the local stories that he knows best and aptly meshes them with the universal. In due course the historical and the local come to a confluence at a remote sanatorium in Southern California, where we witness the appalling lengths that doctors would go to in the name of science. As the world focused its attention on the Second World War that raged across Europe, at the Olive View Sanatorium atrocities of a different kind were being committed, for TB was regarded as a disease of the poor, and the poor were regarded as legitimate specimens for experimentation. As Uncle Roberto reminisces:

> Walking through these buildings with my nephew and great nephew gave me a sense of pride. Frankly, knowing the history of these buildings sheds a completely different perspective on what having tuberculosis was and meant, on what medicine was and has accomplished, on how medicine became abusive, and how the patients, especially those of us who were poor, Mexican and black kept our mouths shut and didn't say a word about what the doctors and nurses did to us. (Morales 2008: 13)

With the vicissitudes of poverty and racism confined to the enclosed space of a medical facility, the sanatorium echoes with the Chicano's class struggle at large. And by combining this microcosm of injustice with an insightful treatment of one of the world's most chronic diseases, *The Captain* reads like an allegory of universal suffering: his novel with the most far-reaching implications to date.

Finally, here in *Little Nation and Other Stories*, the question of Chicano space takes on even more personal meaning for these are stories about his native Montebello in Southern California, where his representation of social inequities hits close to home. In a sense, this collection of short stories reads like a keystone to his earlier works, as it provides a glimpse into what motivates his commitment to a local cause that, so often marked by personal invective, provokes a heated reaction to the ignorance that eclipses the cultural wealth and historical value of his homeland. Morales has warned us before, as in Gurpegui's interview where the novelist states: "I think there is still a lot of anger in me, but yet there is fear of really expressing myself. One of these days I want to come out with a volume that is going to . . . maybe anger people or really shock people" (Gurpegui 1996, 12). *Little Nation* satisfies this criterion. Even those accustomed to the author's customary shock therapy will agree that some of the images projected in these stories reach new heights (or perhaps depths) in their offensive nature. Retracing the violence back to Tenochtitlan in the sixteenth century, the collection begins with the disturbing story of a mother's futile efforts to protect her family from the brutality of the Conquest. In so doing Morales conditions his readers early on with a view to the destruction of all things sacred: hallowed lands, the families that inhabit them and a whole (O)ther culture. Emerging in this opening story are the motifs that remain central throughout the work as a whole. The message that there are potentially curative measures in the wisdom of the ancestors who knew this space (Aztlán) firsthand is implicit, with a focus on the vital connection to nature that was severed when indigenous culture was obliterated. In subsequent stories, this wisdom that connects humankind to its natural surroundings is resurrected by the elders of future generations, only to be erased once again by yet another more modern intruder. From the Conquest to the contemporary barrio warfare of the concluding story, these narratives establish the common theme of a world impoverished by its own greed and ambition, in a space that has seen a recurring cycle of violence. For Quetzali, the Aztec mother roaming a land in ruins with her bewildered children, the best that she can hope for is an impossible promise.

In the second story, it is again the matriarch who plays the central role. There is no struggle against injustice for Mama Concha, though, but rather the fundamental task of inspiring the next generation with a hearty appreciation of family and ancestral land. Specifically, the aging Mama Concha teaches her grandson that the effort to nurture the land for the good of the family and community makes it sacred. It is their humble part of the world where they do divine work. The young narrator's tender bond with his grandmother becomes tantamount to the family's sense of belonging, evoking once again the wisdom of generations past that valued the space of Aztlán. Ultimately, such serene images serve to exacerbate the reader's anxiety when, in the stories that follow, family bonds and Nature itself are so callously destroyed. Indeed, the bitter vilification that taints the greater part of *Little Nation* is not without cause.

This much is clear in the story of "The Gardens of Versailles" where, as the title suggests, vast gardens bloom much to the satisfaction of a Europhile city council. The protagonists are French, their style is classical, their heritage is high culture, but their gardens, like their neighbors in the Simons brickyard, are distinctly Mexican. However, the class struggle here is not between the French immigrants who cultivate these gardens and the neighboring Mexican laborers. In spite of the misguided mayor's interest in displaying Montebello's "Spanish French heritage" to distinguished visitors, the Beaugival Estates—much like the prominent Californio ranches depicted in Morales' historical novels—amount to nothing more than obstacles to Gringo modernization. What follows is a familiar story. Eminent domain, that incontestable prerogative of the reigning authority, is declared in the name of progress. Devout homeowners whose very lives are invested in the land beneath their feet put up a valiant fight. At first the magueys and nopales of the gardens resist incursion—they are vigorous and intractable species, after all—but progress has a way of paving its way over nature.

Set in the present-day, the fourth story, "Prickles," evokes a reading calibrated for the modern grotesque in its exploration of the immoderately foul potential of the human body. Like Prometheus, Dr. Frankenstein stole the power of creation from the gods and breathed life through fire into his monster. Morales, in turn, has engendered such monstrosities as the artiorgans and the split-brain man in *Reto*; gruesome deformities in *Rag Doll*; the Cyclops, Endriago, in *Waiting to Happen*; cannibalistic witches in *The Captain of All These Men of Death*; and now, "Prickles" who, as the name implies, is stricken with a disease that produces thorny tumors all over his head and body. Indeed, he is a monster that only a mother could love. Thus it only stands to reason that this basic need be met by the mother of all Mexicans, the Virgin of Guadalupe. But when She also meets the basic needs demanded by the monster's libido, reactions will undoubtedly vary. At length, Prickles, like Endriago and Frankenstein before him, personifies marginalization, re-awakening the reader to society's obsession with purity and the violent lengths to which it will go to cleanse itself of so-called abnormalities.

That the title story, "Little Nation," should begin with an historical account of the Calvary Cemetery is fitting. Here again, the question of space, most notably the land where generations of Mexicans are laid to rest, is brought to the fore. And it is here that the lead character, Micaela, turns her attention to the burial of yet another innocent victim caught in the crossfire of gang warfare. Local gangs are the obvious perpetrators of the community's suffering in East L.A., but the problem runs deeper. The conflict that emerges between community leaders like Micaela and law enforcement agencies calls to mind the endless class struggle between low-income neighborhoods and the authorities that preserve the system that incarcerates them: a billion-dollar industry dependent on corralling poverty, drugs and crime into the barrio. Or, as the narrator explains:

> In this way [the authorities] justify their positions, their jobs as investigators, patrolmen and prison guards for Los Angeles County. It was no secret that the union representing police and prison guards had contracted the most powerful and influential agencies to protect their interests

within national and state governments. The police and other anti-criminal organizations justified their existence in proportion to the growing crime rates. (Morales 2005: 60)

In effect, the way that Morales portrays the barrio's disadvantaged position in society recalls earlier representations of a heterotopia, where spaces of otherness are crammed together, creating friction and spilling over borders. In the would-be utopia of the City of Angels, the barrio constitutes just such a space of otherness: a necessary unofficial sector, where power is shared between the gangster and the police. It is a perverse system upheld by the social order precisely to allow potentially dangerous energies to play themselves out away from utopia's core. In order for utopia to exist, a counterbalance is required, a dumping ground where it can cleanse itself of the grotesque, of poverty, drugs and violence. Moreover, the dominant system is reinforced by the media frenzy that descends on every murder, eager to make headlines. The news camera serves as utopia's obtrusive eye, as the media acquiesce to the public's need to blame society's ills on the barrio. As in the preceding stories, it is the simulation of living free, implied by the title and represented in the noble efforts of its characters that is ultimately eclipsed by hegemonic forces. What Morales leaves us with in this collection, is a hopeless promise, ghosts that haunt sacred lands, a hidden image of a monster painted in miniature beside his beloved Virgin, the soul of an Indian absorbed into a tree and the mystery of a missing body. These are stories to remind us that while the struggle for space may be met by crushing defeats, the spirit will live on. After all, what is a nation, large or little, without a space to call its own?

And so now we ask, "whither the *topos* of Aztlán?" or "where does an author like Alejandro Morales go from here?" Not surprisingly, his projects currently underway delve further into local stories, promising undoubtedly to garner the attention of his international following. For instance, the second installment of his trilogy—tentatively titled, *The Place of the White Heron*—takes us back to the contentious space of the U.S.-Mexican border. At best, this border zone known to some as "Aztlán" could lead to convergence and diversity, a fertile space of cultural possibilities. And yet, between the American Machine of economic progress and the migrant laborer, the border presents more of an agonizing lesion scraped through the Chicano heartland and abandoned to the pestilence of greed and corruption. To the north a militarized front line stands in defense of the nation's treasures and, to the south, hunger. As in Gloria Anzaldúa's often-cited passage—"The U.S.-Mexican border *es una herida abierta* where the Third World grates against the first and bleeds. And before a scab forms it hemorrhages again, the lifeblood of two worlds merging to form a third country—a border culture" (Anzaldúa 1987: 3)—what characterizes this space is the strikingly imbalanced economic division that reinforces the inequalities of a New World Order that breeds poverty. And nowhere is the economic imbalance more ruthless than at the border itself, where multi-nationals set up their interim maquiladoras to exploit a disadvantaged Mexican work force. Arguably, the only thing worse than poverty is poverty surrounded by abundant wealth: high-tech wealth, drug cartel wealth and the alluring Gringo wealth on the other side. The social costs at the margins of the global economy are staggering, and it is here that Morales fixes his gaze and takes up his pen, chronicling the extremes of injustice in a body of work distinguished by its poignant portrayal of spatial dynamics and social disparities.

Adam Spires
Saint Mary's University

Works Cited

Anzaldúa, Gloria. *Borderlands la Frontera: The New Mestiza*. San Francisco: Aunt Lute Books, 1987.

Foucault, Michel. "Of Other Spaces." *Diacritics* 16.1 (1987): 22–27.

Gurpegui, José Antonio. "Interview with Alejandro Morales." José Antonio Gurpegui ed. *Alejandro Morales: Fiction Past, Present, Future Perfect*. Tempe, AZ: Bilingual Press, 1996. 5-13.

Huxley, Aldous. *Brave New World*. Middlesex: Penguin Books, 1960 [1932].

Kafka, Franz. *The Metamorphosis*. Ed. Stanley Corngold. New York: Bantam Books, 1972 [1915].

Lomelí, Francisco. "Hard-Core Barrio Revisited: Violence, Sex, Drugs, and Videotape Through a Chicano Glass Darkly." Introduction. *Barrio on the Edge / Caras viejas y vino nuevo* by Alejandro Morales. Tempe, AZ: Bilingual Press / Editorial Bilingüe, 1998. 1-21.

Márquez, Antonio. "The Use and Abuse of History in Alejandro Morales' *The Brick People* and *The Rag Doll Plagues*." Ed. José Antonio Gurpegui. *Alejandro Morales: Fiction Past, Present, Future Perfect*. Tempe, AZ: Bilingual Press, 1996. 76-85.

McElroy, Bernard. *Fiction of the Modern Grotesque*. New York: St. Martin's Press, 1989.

Morales, Alejandro. *Barrio on the Edge*. Trans. Francisco Lomelí. Tempe, AZ: Bilingual Press, 1998.

___. *The Brick People*. Houston: Arte Público Press, 1988.

___. *The Captain of All These Men of Death*. Tempe, AZ: Bilingual Press, 2008.

___. *Caras viejas y vino nuevo*. Mexico D.F.: Joaquín Mortiz, 1975.

___. "Dynamic Identities in Heterotopia." Ed. José Antonio Gurpegui. *Alejandro Morales: Fiction Past, Present, Future Perfect*. Tempe, AZ: Bilingual Press, 1996. 14-27.

___. *Pequeña nación*. Phoenix: Orbis Press, 2005.

___. *The Rag Doll Plagues*. Houston: Arte Público Press, 1992.

___. *Reto en el paraíso*. Ypsilanti, MI: Bilingual Press, 1983.

___. *River of Angels*. Houston: Arte Público Press, 2014.

___. *La verdad sin voz*. Mexico D.F.: Joaquín Mortiz, 1979.

___. *Waiting to Happen: The Heterotopian Trilogy*. Volume I. San José: Chusma House, 2001.

Orwell, George. *Nineteen Eighty-Four*. Middlesex: Penguin Books, 1954 [1949].

Spires, Adam. "Writing Acadia and Aztlán: The Novels of Claude LeBouthillier and Alejandro Morales." PhD dissertation, The University of Alberta, 2001.

Quetzali

On the morning of August 13, 1522, one year after the fall of
Tenochtitlan, Xochitl, fifteen, and Cuicatl, her five-year-old
brother, ran out of their house chasing after Quetzali, their
mother. They ran to a nearby temple where Spanish soldiers had
arrived at daybreak with a gang of Indian workers to tear down,
stone by stone, the sacred altar of Centeotl, the corn god. A
week before, Spanish soldiers had taken Cualac, the children's
father, to forced-labor corrals in the city. The children held their
mother's hand and with wide, curious eyes watched the destruction of one of the most sacred and honored structures of their
young lives. They watched a Tlamatini, an elder priest, place
himself between the soldiers and the temple and cry out to the
gods to stop the Spanish advance. While the priest prayed to
protect the sacred shrine, the Spanish infantrymen dropped their
lances to their hips and pushed the long steel-bladed pikes into
the priest and several others who defended the temple. The
Tlamatini, trying to pull the lance from his body, writhed in
pain like a decapitated serpent staining its holy feathers with
blood and dirt. Suddenly, from the interior of the temple a second Tlamatini, carrying a sacred image, bolted out and
attempted to break away from the Spanish soldiers. The holy
man was captured and forced to his knees. The Spaniard in
charge, who carried a blunderbuss at his side, ordered the
Tlamatini to stand. He then raised the stone image above his

1

head and slammed it to the ground, thus shattering the mighty Centeotl at the feet of Xochitl and Cuicatl who, paralyzed with fear, now only recognized fragments of the god's face. For an instant the children's and the soldier's eyes met. The soldier's vision encompassed them, lingered on Xochitl and Quetzali. He calmly turned to one of the Tlamatini, grabbed the blunderbuss and fired directly into the *sabio*'s face. Quetzali screamed and shielded Xochitl and Cuicatl's eyes from the sight of two dying holy men.

But it was too late. The girl and her brother watched the once-powerful, magical Tlamatinime flailing on the yellowish soil. Chunks of the holy man's face landed on the equally dismembered pieces of Centeotl. The children carefully followed the priest's blood flowing toward them. As the blood surrounded the children, the Spanish soldier reloaded the blunderbuss, holstered it on a leather saddle and mounted a restless horse. Horrified, Quetzali and her children attempted to run back to their house, but natural and unnatural forces frustrated their escape. Now, the number of Indian workers had grown and completely covered the temple. They crawled over every sacred space and methodically, stone by stone, deconstructed it. More soldiers arrived, and several blocked Quetzali's path. The three—Quetzali, Xochitl and Cuicatl—were forced to witness the complete destruction of the shrine.

The soldiers wore a colorful red uniform. Layers of leather covered the chest and abdomen. They wielded long lethal pikes, heavy swords, daggers and a few blunderbusses. Metal helmets and armor protected them from what arms the Indians might still possess. The children were terrified and intrigued by the uniformed soldiers who swiftly and mercilessly acted upon the Indian men. Being bright, observant children, they noticed how the once-powerful Aztec warriors, respected Pochteca, sacred Tlatoani and scholarly Tlamatini responded immediately to the soldiers' gestures and commands. Brutality countered any hesitation, conquered any hint of resistance. An Indian who stepped out of line or failed to work effectively disappeared. He was sent far away to work, the soldiers explained to the families searching for their loved ones.

The power to command and to make the Indian men respond immediately and without question or complaint, only a year ago, had been in the mouths and hands of Tlatoani, Tlamatinime, Pipiltín and Aztec warriors. But for Xochitl and Cuicatl, like Quetzali who had protected them while the battles were being fought, while the army of strangers came nearer to their village, it was only that morning that the children understood that their world was crumbling and that a great change was occurring. The children now saw Aztec warriors made into slaves, beaten and forced to destroy the temples of the once-powerful gods central to their lives and community, and now unable to defend themselves and their faithful people. Spanish soldiers ordered Aztec men to throw the bodies of the Tlamatinime on the mounds of broken sacrificial stones. Power, it was clear, was now in the hands of the Spaniards, for it was they who now decided who was to be sacrificed.

The children watched the Spanish soldiers and observed the Indian work crew take down a temple wall and push down a second. By the late afternoon only the base, a small pyramid, was all that was left of the temple. There came a pause in the work. The Spaniards, the Indian workers and the villagers who lived in the area were brought together and made to wait. For a long while, nobody moved. All human activity on Earth had ceased for rest and prayer. Finally, a man wearing long robes and escorted by soldiers climbed the small pyramid and directed the building of a pyre around the Tlamatinime. The robed man raised his hands to the sky, and the children and their mother were made to kneel and bow their heads. The few who did not understand the example were clubbed to their knees. From the pyramid the robed man pronounced strange words to which the soldiers replied with sounds and odd movements of the right hand touching the forehead, the abdomen, the left shoulder, the right shoulder and the lips. The man with long robes motioned for the people to rise. While the children tightly held their mother's hand, fire consumed the bodies of the Aztec Tlamatinime. The foulness of burning hair and flesh floated beyond the village and rose to the sacred mountains of the Valley of Anahuac.

The soldiers and the robed man seemed satisfied and ordered the Indian work gang to march in a column back to Tenochtitlan, to where thousands of Indians lived corralled for months. The Indian men formed a long procession in the same direction where Cualac had been taken weeks before. Early in the day, the reason Quetzali had rushed to the temple was to see if her husband was among the work crew. The children waited while their mother, crying softly, with reddened eyes tired with worry, looked at each one of the men as they filed past, but her husband was not among them. Now, in the late afternoon, without a word, Quetzali nudged her children gently forward and added herself, her daughter and her son to the end of the column.

At first, the Spanish soldiers guarding the end of the long chain of Indians did not pay much attention to the woman, the girl and the boy who had joined the line. After a while the soldiers noticed the women and began to talk to Quetzali and Xochitl. The soldiers laughed and ran between Quetzali and Xochitl and tried to separate them from Cuicatl. Holding on to her children, Quetzali fell to the ground and screamed. The soldier with the blunderbuss retreated from the head of the procession to where Quetzali continued to scream. The soldier ordered the infantrymen to move on. For a short while he looked down at the family. Then he fixed his eyes on Xochitl, who sat calmly next to her screaming mother. In silence he waited until Quetzali halted her cries, and then he finally rode away.

At sunset Quetzali, Xochitl and Cuicatl found themselves outside the walls of the palace of the former lord of Coyoacan that was now occupied by Cortés, the leader of the Spanish troops who had destroyed Tenochtitlan. In the distance large fires burned and columns of smoke rose above the great city. Quetzali would not return home, for she was afraid that the gods no longer protected her and her family. She carried Cuicatl, held Xochitl's hand and moved on, determined to find her husband. Late that night, exhaustion overwhelmed them. They huddled together and slept on the side of the grand causeway leading into the ritual center of the city.

The morning chill and the ringing of bells awakened Quetzali to the sight of an Indian work gang heading out toward Coyoacan. Quetzali again waited until all the men had passed. Her husband was not one of them. She roused the children, and they headed to the center of the city. As they neared the center, chaos and frenzy dominated the movement of Indian men, women and children. Armed Spanish soldiers guarded every crossroad and patrolled every street. Quetzali remembered how months earlier, carts full of Indian bodies were driven out of the city for burial. Quetzali noticed that the Spaniards had cleared the rubble from the demolished holy places and leveled most of the Aztec sacred monuments. The calpulli temples, the calmecac, the telpochtlatoque and the amoxcalli had been obliterated. Stores, Indian peddlers and medical practitioners no longer advertised their services. The central market next to the ritual precinct had disappeared. How radically the city had changed in a matter of months, Quetzali thought as she moved forward.

Finally, she stood before the twin-towered pyramid of Tlaloc and Huitzilopochtli, but it was barely recognizable. The towers were gone. Indian work crews took stones from the top

of the pyramid and moved them to other parts of the city. Where
the grandeur of the Indian city had once resided, Cortés started
to rebuild what he envisioned as the most imposing and powerful city in the New World. Quetzali, Xochitl and Cuicatl, each
in their own manner, grasped that all Indian material and meta-
physical entities had fallen and were quickly disappearing.

After the fall of the city, the relationship between Spaniard
and Aztec was that of the victor and the vanquished. The real
king-god of Mexico was no longer Moctezuma or Cuauhtemoc,
no longer Indian, but now it was Cortés, and by being appoint-
ed Viceroy, in the eyes of the Indians, he stayed king to the end.
No other Spaniard ever received such hatred, obedience and
adulation. Cortés living in Coyoacan remained the one authen-
tic "teule" or god.

Quetzali followed the road to the north of the ritual center.
The scent of ash reminded her that the Aztec dwellings that had
once dominated the area had met the same fate as the temple in
her town. While Quetzali walked, lost in thought with her arms
on her children's shoulders, an image of a corral, a short distance away, with thousands of men and women waiting, formed
in her sight. These people were prisoners destined to be labor
slaves. Quetzali ran toward the corral in hopes of finding her
husband, but saw soldiers clubbing half-naked Indian women in
tattered garments. The soldiers opened the women's skirts and
ripped their upper garments. They felt everywhere: their hair,
their ears and their breasts. They made the women raise their
skirts and inspected them between their thighs. Some women
were taken away and others were pushed into the corral. At
another gate, soldiers beat the men and ripped their clothes off,
lowered their loincloths and tore from their bodies gold ear-
rings, nose and lip plugs, necklaces, bracelets and hair
ornaments. Robed men directed this activity. Quetzali now
understood that the robed men were the conquerors' priests.

Xochitl and Cuicatl witnessed Indian women brutally abused and warriors stripped and beaten. Raped of their human identity, the Aztecs were rendered objects of possession. Quetzali saw a third gate where Indian men were being organized in work gangs. As the men exited the corral, the soldiers haphazardly branded them on the face and pushed them to where a priest handed out clothes to cover their bodies. As this was happening, Quetzali recognized a neighbor's son. The young man saw her, but from the turn of his angry face she understood that she had to flee.

Quickly, Quetzali, Xochitl and Cuicatl retreated into a narrow street that ran to the west of the city. After a while they heard many voices singing. They came upon a three-walled structure covered with maguey leaves. There under the roof and at the center, a Spanish priest stood in front of an altar, while a man with a crown of thorns nailed to a huge wooden cross towered above him. The priest prayed and sang to hundreds of Indians who were on their knees, with their heads bowed and all dressed exactly alike. Several of the Indians looked up and caught Quetzali's and the children's gaze. A sudden sense of distance, of difference and of sorrow was communicated between those Indians, who were on their knees, and Quetzali, Xochitl and Cuicatl, who were still standing. But a quick expression from the face of a kneeling woman told Quetzali to run away. She heard soldiers coming. She now recognized the special noise their spiked boots and weapons made and the sound of the horse hooves on the stone streets, a sound never to be forgotten. Xochitl and Cuicatl followed their mother as she walked quickly down a long, narrow corridor between two buildings that opened to a garden where several groups of handsome young Indian men were learning the Christian tongue. Several robed men directed the groups, who at that instant all turned to see the intruders. There was a profound silence followed by great laughter. A robed man approached, beckoning them to come closer. Quetzali stepped back and, as fast as she could run, led her children out of the garden. Only laughter pursued them.

Hours later, as Huitzilopochtli descended to the underworld, Quetzali, Xochitl and Cuicatl were retracing steps back home, resting near the causeway to Coyoacan. They hid in a field of maguey and cactus where Quetzali started to beat her chest violently. She had neglected her children. They had neither eaten nor drunk water for nearly two days, nor had they complained. In her urgency to find her husband, Cualac, she had neglected their care; she had acted egregiously against her innocents. She beat her breast until Xochitl grabbed one hand to stop her. Cuicatl held the other hand and smiled whimsically. Quetzali embraced them both and, although they were hungry and thirsty, the three slept throughout the night until Huitzilopochtli opened their eyes.

On that sunny morning, Quetzali's first thought upon returning to her house and smoldering village was where she would get food for her children. While most houses had been destroyed, a few, although badly damaged, were still standing. She looked about, but nobody came out to help. Her village was abandoned. Her only hope now to find food and water was the Monte. There, she and the children might find fruits, herbs and roots to eat, water inside particular plants, and maybe a stream. She resigned to surrender herself and her children to the fate of the energies of nature. Desperate, she hugged Xochitl and Cuicatl and bravely moved into the forest. However, only a few steps into the natural green canopy, a scream and muffled voices halted their advance to safety, food and water. The forest had been invaded by the soldiers who had burned her village. She moved to the side of the path and, below her, saw in an arroyo five soldiers with three Indian women. They forced the Indian women to drink from a bladder and stripped them. One soldier removed his boots and pants and approached one of the women. Quetzali, Xochitl and Cuicatl returned to the path. She heard a noise up ahead and turned back to the burned village. Back in the open area of the village, free from the forest, the noise that she had heard came closer. It was a horse. The nape of her back turned ice cold, and she shivered from fear and hatred of the beast and its rider directly behind her. Suddenly, the sound of a loud explosion, a blunderbuss fired above their heads, knocked them to the ground.

The soldier with the blunderbuss had returned. He dismounted and walked toward Quetzali and Xochitl. Quetzali ordered her children to run, but they remained by her side. They stayed, waited defiantly and shielded their mother. The soldier hoisted the blunderbuss over his shoulder and took Xochitl. Quetzali ran to the soldier and swung, striking his heavy leather vest. He pushed her and Cuicatl to the burned earth. With Xochitl screaming for her mother, he mounted the horse and struck Xochitl several times in the mouth. With Xochitl in his grasp, he pulled the reins and turned to face Quetzali and Cuicatl. For a moment, the boy, although sobbing, caught the soldier's eye. The boy fixed his gaze sharply and profoundly into the Spanish soldier's pupil. The soldier rode off in the direction of the city.

By midday, Quetzali and Cuicatl found themselves in the middle of their world's ashes, now being whirled, played with and teased by the wind. Quetzali raised her eyes to Huitzilopochtli and wished that he had not come back. Cuicatl traced figures of animals on the black ground. She never heard the cries of the women in the forest or the soldiers riding away. She figured that they had gone deeper into the arroyo. She felt faint and weak. A constant pain seared her stomach. Cuicatl had covered his face with ash. His hands and feet were black. He never complained or asked for food or water. Finally, she moved under the shade of a tree and closed her eyes. When she opened them, one of her neighbors, an old woman, stood before her. She offered them a tortilla and water. The old woman, silent, spoke with her hands, fluttering her fingers and moving her arms, saying that the people of the village had dispersed in many directions and they would never return.

The following morning Quetzali and Cuicatl traveled the road leading back to Coyoacan and into the city in a vain search for their loved ones. Quetzali and Cuicatl wandered for two days without eating. Instead of offering to help, like they would have before the coming of the Spanish soldiers, her people shied away from Quetzali and her son. When she asked for the whereabouts of Xochitl or Cualac, none of her people offered any information. A fear gripped the Aztec people, and the tradition of helping neighbors in need was replaced by suspicion and a tendency to hoard material food and water. On the third day of searching, Quetzali and Cuicatl found themselves back at the plaza where the Christian priest led the Indians in prayer and song, and taught them the Spanish language. There she left Cuicatl, not with a priest but with an Indian woman dressed in Spanish garments. To distract Cuicatl, the Indian woman offered the boy a papaya. "I love you, I'll be back for you, I must find Xochitl and your father." For a moment, Quetzali watched her son eat. She silently said goodbye, pledging her love and her promise to return, and disappeared into the shadow of the crumbling temple walls.

Mama Concha

My first and perhaps only memories of my grandmother Mama Concha were of the vast fields where we lived on the outskirts of Los Angeles. Our properties were close enough that I could walk to my grandparents' house. My house wasn't big, but the land where it was built appeared to me back then to be long and wide. My parents and especially my grandfather, who came to live with us after Mama Concha died, loved to plant vegetable gardens, fruit trees and small parcels of corn and sugar cane. We also had chickens, goats and dozens of rabbits. I would always follow my grandfather around whenever he worked in the garden, fed the animals or when he slaughtered a chicken or rabbit for supper. I was about four years old when my father began to help with the slaughtering. I began to realize that my little grandfather, who once had hands like bear paws, was finding it more difficult to keep the animals from squirming free. Whenever a chicken or rabbit escaped the chopping block, he would get mad and start yelling a bunch of bad words that would bring my father out to calm him down. My grandfather was already very old, and he spent his days reliving his memories. In the evenings, as the sun set and the air was refreshed by a gentle breeze, I would see him sitting under one of the quince trees. Here he would tell me stories about my grandmother. He cried a lot because he missed her, and he

would say that he couldn't live without her. This always frightened me because I didn't want to lose my grandfather, too.

From what I remember about Mama Concha, I would
always see her picking fruit or carrying fruit up to the house or
preparing it for mealtime. She had a special way with grandfather's strawberries. I got to help her harvest them, filling a
basket for the whole family. I felt proud to be able to help my
grandmother, and I insisted on carrying the basket which would
be so full of big, juicy red berries that I couldn't see in front of
me. So I walked sideways with my eyes fixed steadily on the
path. My grandmother followed patiently behind, right up until
I lifted the basket up onto the kitchen table. She made me wash
my hands before picking out the best strawberries, which was
hard to do because they all looked so scrumptious. I washed
them and put them in a big bowl. She would bring out a knife,
cutting board and mortar. She placed a dozen or so strawberries
on the cutting board, removed the stems and tips, then cut them
into four pieces. She did this with all but the last dozen berries,
which she cut into halves for her strawberry broth. She placed
the mortar into a large dish. With both hands she scooped up a
pile of freshly cut strawberries and piled them into the hollow
of the mortar, where she crushed them with a stone pestle.
When she was finished she added the sugar.

"Go fetch a spoon and try some."

The crushed strawberries tasted sweet and fresh. Then she
placed three bananas on the cutting board, cut them into half-
inch pieces and added them to the crushed strawberries.

"Let's see if you like bananas."

I opened my mouth wide and grandmother fed me the
strawberries with a small piece of banana floating in the red
juice.

"I like them, Grandmother!"

She returned with a round piece of bread in the middle of a small dish. She smothered the bread with the strawberry-banana puree and topped it off with whipped cream.

"There, love. You learn to appreciate strawberries after the work you put into them."

I hugged Mama Concha, who pulled me onto her lap and curled me up between her breasts. That was my favorite place, sitting on her lap and breathing in the scent of my grandmother.

That's how I remember her: big and strong. I breathed her strength. I was sure that Mama Concha was a powerful woman because everyone in the family paid attention to her and obeyed whatever she said. Even Grandfather knew not to argue with her. That's why he would sometimes wander off, afraid that Concha was getting riled up about something. My most vivid memory that to this day I relive in my dreams is picturing her amid the big fruit trees in the garden. Grandfather had planted pomegranate trees, guava, apricot and plum trees. There were also two large avocado trees that were growing in the garden naturally. I loved my grandmother. And though I didn't realize it then, I learned a great deal from her wisdom.

🐞 🐞 🐞

Mama Concha wore the fragrance of the fruits she harvested and prepared. If she picked guavas, which have a very strong aroma, it stayed with her for a long time.

"Guava is a big sumptuous fruit!"

She held two handfuls up to my nose.

"Fragrance is a passion, my child."

She picked out a big guava and cleaned it on her apron. She rolled it around in her fingers.

"Look at the peel. It's a soft smooth green. Smell the sweetness that invites you to cut it open like this."

Grandmother sliced the guava in two.

"Notice the pink color of the flesh, so light and appealing like a soft perfume, inviting you to savor its sweetness, slowly, unlike a crunchy apple that you have to bite into firmly. No. Not like that, Child. The guava is delicate. You eat it slowly, tenderly."

She told me this because the guavas were so good that she didn't want me to eat too many and end up with a stomachache. Grandmother made jam with the guavas and gave some to the whole family and her neighborhood friends.

🐞 🐞 🐞

Grandmother had big apricot trees. She liked to sit on a bench under her favorite one, and I would often sit with her to keep her company. We cuddled up close together. I hugged her and breathed deeply, assured that she emanated a wonderful fragrance of love. I told her so, which brought a big smile to her face that warmed my heart. Often we just sat in silence.

"Listen to the stillness."

Little by little I learned to listen for silence. For the most part I didn't hear anything, but I imagined an empty quiet space where I drifted into tranquil slumber beside my grandmother.

The apricots were big, of an orangey yellow color. Grandmother picked the ripe ones and filled a basket that she set down between us.

"Look at the lovely color. This one has just ripened."

She wiped it on her apron, and with her thick fingers she split it open into halves.

"Notice the pit, how dark it is, the apricot's seed. Be careful not to eat it by mistake. We enjoy the fruit so much that we sometimes forget that it has a pit. If we don't pay attention, we could choke on it. This little pit is the seed, the heart and womb of the tree, and it can grow up big just like one of these enormous trees. Just remember that it can hurt you if you don't respect it when you eat the fruit. Now look at the color of the flesh."

I realized that it was almost the same color as the skin. Grandmother raised the apricot to my mouth for me to taste it. She smiled when she saw the look of surprise on my face.

"It's so sweet, Mama Concha."

"Well, of course! Mama Concha picks only the best for her handsome little boy."

I felt very comfortable at her feet, snuggled up against her legs or holding on to her apron. I was safe there, under her favorite tree, listening to the birds, watching the dog, the cat, all the hens and the goats. You could see the rabbit cages from where we were sitting.

I could tell that everyone loved Grandmother very much because neighbors would often come to visit her, or relatives who lived far away would travel to see her. They, too, would sit with her on her bench. At her feet I would look up at these friends and relatives who seemed to laugh a lot together or sometimes cried with her. I remember that in the mornings for breakfast Mama Concha gave me toast with apricot jam. She thought that apricot jam was the easiest to spread, but I preferred the jams with pieces of fruit in them. They were the sweetest, and she didn't mind if I left the little pieces on the table or dropped them on the floor.

🐞 🐞 🐞

"This plot of land is our place in the world. We take only what we need. There's no need to ask for more than our share."

There were other trees on their land that also produced fruit, but none that I liked as much as her favorite apricot tree. Mama

Concha knew which fruits I liked but made me try them all. One was the sapodilla plum, which grew on gigantic trees. Those were the biggest trees on my grandparents' property. I think that many of the trees had been there for a long time, planted years and years before. My grandmother used to explain that the trees, the gardens and all the work that my family put into it—all that effort—is what made the land sacred.

"Ancient, this place is ancient. It's our part of the world, our share of the land to do God's work."

The sapodilla plum has green skin and an inside that's as white as snow, my grandmother told me. I don't think that she ever really saw snow except for the distant mountain tops that received a white covering every winter. I would wake up one morning and the mountain tops were white. In the mornings I went looking for Grandmother in the kitchen where she prepared coffee for Grandfather and my parents. On those first days of winter Mama Concha would scoop me up in her arms and take me outside where she'd point toward the mountains.

"Look at the snow, white, white on the mountains. It must be so clean and cold up there, and pretty."

I wanted so much to see the snow up close, to touch and feel it with my hands. It was Mama Concha who had showed it to me for the first time. She held me against her chest and, with her finger, she traced the snow line along the distant mountains.

The sapodilla plum meant it was winter. In our warm cozy kitchen, Grandmother was eating a sapodilla and nut jam that I didn't much care for.

"Have a little bit more of the jam, child. Learn to appreciate all that God has given us."

My grandparents really liked the sapodilla jam. They served it to all the old folks around Simons, because I think they were the only ones who would eat the stuff. It's that the sapodilla plum was the only fruit that I feared. I remember once when

three of Mama Concha's friends came to pick up a few baskets
of sapodillas that she had set aside for them. The women sat at
the kitchen table where I was taking the smallest of bites of my
bread with sapodilla jam. Mama Concha served them coffee
and also some of the jam with bread. The women started talking about how they were going to use the sapodillas.

"We don't make jams like you do, Concha."

"Concha, you'll make a jam out of any fruit."

They all laughed.

"You know what we do with the sapodilla plums you give
us? We use them for a skin ointment to reduce brown patches
and to fight infections. And another use is for sore thighs and
aching bones."

"It's good for rheumatism," another friend added.

"And you know we're going to send our grandchildren out
to collect more when we start using the seeds. We'll take as
many as you can give us, Concha."

"If you wish, you can take them all. Pick the ones from the
ground first, and then you can take them off the tree. But be
very careful because it's an enormous tree. And come as soon
as you can because the fallen ones will begin to rot."

"Thank you, Concha," said the eldest. "We'll start this week
with the soporific and the sedative that we prepare every year.
We'll make more than last year because we were sold out
before the end of the year."

"We've got to prepare more sedative because it helps the
nerves, and it's good for calming tiresome kids, and for insom-
niacs."

"But be careful, as the seeds can be poisonous, depending
on how you prepare them," Mama Concha warned.

"Not to worry, Concha, we know very well how to prepare
these medications, as well as the poison. It's good for killing

rats and moles, and larger animals. Not to worry, Concha. We are much obliged for the use of your fruit."

"Well, thanks to all of you for using up the sapodilla plums, because when they begin to rot they bring swarms of flies. That's why Eutimio wants to cut those trees down. I won't let him, though. When I'm dead he can do whatever he wishes with all of this.

Mama Concha noticed the look of fright in my expression. When I heard that the seeds were poisonous and that she was going to die, I was done with eating sapodilla jam.

"No, Grandson, I'm not going to die tomorrow."

"Of course not. Your grandmother will live for many years."

The eldest got up from the table.

"We've got to be going, Concha. We're going to go see Lidia, your neighbor, the one who lives in the last house on the street. She has an uncle who suffers from insomnia. They called and asked us to come over this afternoon."

My grandmother's friends left, and all was quiet in the kitchen as I sat at the table with still half a slice of bread and jam in my hand. Grandmother made me a hot tea.

"Here, drink this. It'll make you feel better."

I didn't want any.

"It's not the same tea that the ladies were drinking," Mama Concha assured me with a little smile.

Later on I went outside to see the sapodilla tree that now had a mysterious meaning for me. I stood beneath the immense tree and it beckoned for me to climb it, right to the very top. But I couldn't reach even the lowest branches.

🐜 🐜 🐜

The pomegranate trees were at the back of the property. It wasn't far, but Mama Concha was taking her time. She brought a basket, and I was carrying a wooden chair for her. It was hard to carry because it was almost as big as I was. A few times I had to just drag it. I carried it against my chest, on my back and on my head like a crown. The pomegranate trees weren't very big. There were about six of them that produced a pile of fruit. Grandmother pointed to the tree where she wanted me to put the chair. I set it up, and she sat down.

"Fill the basket for me, Grandson. Make sure that they're bigger than apples. And look at the skin. It should be firm and tight like a dried animal hide."

I didn't quite understand what she meant, but I held the pomegranates and asked her:

"Is this a good one? Should I pick it?"

I don't think that Grandmother really saw the pomegranates I was showing her, but she always answered back.

"Yes, yes. Make sure it has little whiskers around the bottom."

I liked how red it was, and pink in places. A lot of them had both colors. It wasn't easy to pluck them off. I pulled and twisted each one until the fruit detached from the branch. Sometimes the branch would break and I would fall to the ground, branch in hand.

"Gracious, be careful with that tree."

I sat by her side to see which pomegranate she was choosing from the basket. Grandmother would lift one up, look it over, squeeze it and, with all her might, plunge her finger tips into the bottom. Then, by rotating her hands in opposite directions, she would tear the fruit in two, which popped like a small gunshot. I was left with my mouth gaping at how strong she was. I tried to do the same, but my hands got tired from trying to break the skin with my fingers.

One afternoon my grandmother and I went to pick pomegranates to make a kind of syrup, like a jam and juice. This time she didn't make me bring a chair, but instead an old blanket. We filled two big bags and then sat down to eat. Again she split them in two with her fingers, handing me a half piece.

"Look at how the insides of the pomegranate are so well organized. So many thin little bags of red seeds, like rubies filled with red juice."

Grandmother tore off some more pieces of pomegranate for me.

"Now you can enjoy eating one ruby at a time or bite into fifty juicy rubies all at once."

First I started separating the seeds until I had a little pile of them that I could savor one by one. Then when I ate them by the handful, the juice ran out from the corners of my mouth, staining the white T-shirt I was wearing. Grandmother noticed how I had dripped juice down the front of my shirt and laughed.

"It looks like you're wearing a bib!"

She burst out laughing. Never before had I seen her laugh so hard that her whole body shook. I felt that laughter in my heart, and it filled me with happiness. I stared at my hands and T-shirt all covered in red. I looked up at Grandmother and shared in her laughter. She was so happy that I couldn't help but feel the same way. She put her arm around me, and I noticed how her flabby skin hung down. By those days Grandmother had begun to swell up in her arms, legs and waist. While I observed how big my laughing grandmother was, my mother came running over.

"What happened? How did you cut yourself?"

Then she realized that it wasn't blood but rather the crimson juice of the pomegranate rubies we were devouring. She pulled me up by the arm and dragged me off toward the house.

"Concha! Would you just look at this child!"

"Now calm down, Juanita. It's not the fault of my handsome boy who I love so much. Just leave him to me."

"You should be resting. Not out here eating pomegranates!"

"Oh, but you're wrong, Juanita. What time I have left I want to spend with my grandchildren."

My mother took me straight to the bathtub to clean me up.

🐞 🐞 🐞

The next time that I saw Mama Concha was under a white light that shone down on a tree. I couldn't tell where it was coming from except that it was from way up high. She was wearing a pretty dress, a thin black fabric with a pattern of little white flowers woven tightly together. A gold necklace adorned her thick neck. I saw that she was watching me from behind little branches of white flowers that made a crown for her head and danced before her smiling face. My Mama Concha looked very pretty underneath that shower of light and snow-white flowers. Radiant shafts of light from the heavens glorified her like a queen. She was an angel, my queen of heavenly angels. I walked toward her. I couldn't make out all of her face, but I knew that it was Grandmother underneath that tree of cascading white flowers and brilliant light that formed a transparent veil, a protective barrier that I couldn't cross at that moment. I am certain that she saw me walking toward her. With my outstretched hand I gently parted the veil of light and flowers. In that warm and tender glow where millions of flowers danced and floated to the ground, ashen petals the color of her hair, that's where I found my Mama Concha, who took me into her arms and kissed me. Together we laughed in a celebration of transparent whiteness, intense and vivid light that sheltered us under the tree.

🐞 🐞 🐞

Weeks went by, then months. Little by little I noticed that Mama Concha wasn't getting out as often as before. I would wait for her on the little bench under the nearest apricot tree, but she never came out to talk about the trees or eat any fruit. I found myself wondering why she needed so much rest. One day when I was coming home from school I saw that there were two cars parked in front of the house. I went and sat on the steps of the little porch that faced the dirt road. I could hear my mother talking with neighbors and with some people who spoke English. My mother could make herself understood in English, unlike my father, who could barely say "thank you" or "good morning." I could hear them but I didn't understand what they were saying about Mama Concha. I got up and moved away from the door because they were coming out. I recognized Dr. Walland and the nurse who worked in his office. They said hello to me and then drove off in their cars. That was the first time it dawned on me that something was wrong with Grandmother.

After Dr. Walland's visit, who was also my doctor, my aunt and uncle took Grandmother to see him, and then they took her to the hospital, and she stayed there for four days. When she came back home she asked my mother to let her go outside to sit under the apricot tree that was nearest the house. Mama Concha wanted to have her body warmed by the sun. We were so happy to see her at peace outside instead of lying in bed. Before going to school I went by her room to see her, but she was in the kitchen with Grandfather. They were talking in hushed voices. I hadn't seen them together like that in a long time. They both hugged me and blessed me. That morning I ran to school and I saw that the trees didn't seem quite as big as before. In a year or two I would be able to reach the lowest branches.

In the following days Mama Concha struggled to get out of bed to come outside with me. She could sit for an hour or so under the apricot tree. I looked after her, ready to run inside to get Mother if my grandmother didn't feel well. We talked about the weather, the sky, the sun and clouds, and the warm caress of the afternoon breeze. I liked it when all of a sudden she raised her hand.

"Silence. Just listen to it!"

I snuggled in behind her big arms, which Mother said were very swollen, and I made an enormous effort to remain quiet so that I could hear every possible sound that inhabited the space that Grandmother and I were sharing. We stayed like that for a long while, not even blinking, until I could hear the beating of her heart. And I'm sure that she could hear mine. Our two hearts beat as one, and I knew that she was taking in my energy and spirit to find strength.

"Juanita, children are the source of strength and energy for the family."

In her arms I understood what she was trying to say to my mother. I pulled my head away from her chest and for the first time I saw tears welled up in her eyes. She quickly pulled me back against her bosom and held me tight, trying to hide her sobbing. I had to accept that Mama Concha was sick, and I realized that she needed my help. She depended on my strength, energy and spirit to go on living.

In the mornings I would go to her room to see how she was doing, but her neighborhood friends wouldn't let me disturb her if she was still sleeping. I would go back to see her after school. Sometimes she'd accompany me outside, but she could no longer stroll among the trees, not even to her favorite apricot tree. Mother started taking her out in a wheelchair, one that Dr. Walland had brought over. One afternoon Mother allowed me to take her outside, but barely twenty minutes had passed before she got tired and asked me to bring her back to the house.

"Mama Concha, tomorrow after school I'll take you to see all the trees, the gardens and the vegetable patch that Grandfather planted."

"We'll see if I can, my dear child. Let your mother know. I'll wait for you tomorrow afternoon."

I pushed her inside using the ramp that my father and grandfather had built. She wasn't as heavy as I thought she would be. Holding the door open for us, Mother had overheard my plan to take Mama Concha out to see the trees.

"We'll see how your grandmother feels tomorrow. If she's well enough, you can take her just past the apricot tree."

"Yes, one tree at a time. I'm not sure if I can handle visiting all of them at once." Mama Concha chuckled. Mother took her back to her room. As I was leaving, the neighbors came in, Grandmother's friends. I stepped off to the side so that they wouldn't see me. They walked in without greeting anyone and went straight to Grandmother's room.

"Juanita, we're here to help Concha with her bath," one of her friends announced in a loud voice.

"We've brought something for the pain," the oldest of them yelled out.

Grandmother spent a whole week resting before she was able to come outside with me to see the trees and Grandfather's little corn fields. He had cleaned off the path that we always took. Grandfather came with us this time, and he pushed the wheelchair. I felt proud to be walking with Mama Concha and Papa Timo, and I could tell that they really enjoyed that afternoon under the pomegranate trees, the ones farthest from the house. We had no trouble making it to the edge of the grove because Papa Timo had done such a good job leveling the path that went around the whole property. When we finished our walk, we left Mama Concha with Mother, who took her back to her room with the help of a few friends. Before she went in,

Grandmother gave me a kiss and a blessing. From inside she raised her hand toward me and made her fingers dance a little goodbye.

🐜 🐜 🐜

Three weeks passed without any more visits with Mama Concha. Mother wouldn't let me see her. It was always the wrong time. Now Grandfather was constantly going to her room. My brothers and sisters came to see her. Aunts and uncles would come to visit, then leave in tears. Dr. Walland came every three days, and the nurse came when he couldn't be there. He was a really good doctor, the only one who would treat patients from the barrio. He and the nurse talked a lot with Mother. They gave her instructions about how to administer Grandmother's medicine, and how to slow the hemorrhaging.

One morning Mother and two friends were in Mama Concha's room and, when one of them went out to the kitchen, the door was left open. No one realized that I had come in and hid myself in a corner where I could see what they were doing to Grandmother. Mama Concha was lying on her back, her head turned away from me. Mother swiftly pulled long cloths out from between Mama Concha's legs and tossed them into a bucket. The cloths were white and warm with steam, but they were soaked in places with a dark crimson, like the ruby red juice of a burst pomegranate.

The Gardens of Versailles

For Carlos

*. . . later a mule driver told me that it's not arriving
first that matters. It's knowing how to get there.*

—El rey

No one knew for sure where he came from. By the early
1920s, when these parts were made up of ranches and farm-
land worked by Mexicans and the Japanese, Plácido Beaugival
had already settled near Simons. Beaugival (everyone around
here just called him Beaugival) said that he was French. He had
a wife, but she rarely left the house. Whenever we asked about
her he would just say that she stayed home because she didn't
speak Spanish or English. He would explain that his wife *"ne
parle que français,"* and that he was the only person around
here who spoke French.

I remember seeing her out in public on only two occasions.
The first time was when her brother visited from Mexico. He
was a young man, short, with messy hair over his square-shaped
head, a veritable Napoleon. He spent his nights at the cantinas
near Simons, especially on paydays when more women came
out and the place was bustling. The second time was when she
emerged from the house elegantly dressed, strutting like a pea-
cock with all the stately posture of royalty, shoulder to shoulder

27

with her husband in defiance of the construction workers and the
enormous bulldozers that devoured the earth before them.
Strangely, I never did find out her first name. She was known
simply as "La Beaugival." You would hear her voice more than
you would ever see her. Many times, as I wandered by the house,
I could hear La Beaugival playing the piano and singing her
beloved French songs, often accompanied by her husband:

Tu pars, et je vais languir
Dans les regrets et les désirs.
Je languirai jusqu'au soir.

We would see Beaugival returning from work carrying two
or three potted plants, destined for the vast gardens that they
tended in back of the house. These were the Gardens of
Versailles. Though private, everyone from Simons spoke about
how beautiful they were, describing them as if they themselves
had seen them, as if they had strolled along the paths, but the
truth was that only the Beaugivals knew these gardens.

They fenced off the terrain on three sides with cactuses and
maguey plants that, over time, filled with thorns, spiders and
snakes. I remember once when the cactuses yielded such an
abundant crop of prickly pears that Beaugival asked us to take
as many as we wanted. Inside, stretching along the dense
foliage, there stood thick brick walls embedded with nails and
shards of glass. This is how they protected their privacy. They
would smile at the friends and neighbors who went by the house
admiring the gardens, fully aware that it was forbidden to enter.

To show just how much he loved his wife, Beaugival built
their home with his own bare hands. But instead of Simons
brick, he used blocks of adobe, which were more efficient at
cooling the house in the summer and keeping in the heat during
the winter months. He apologized to us Simons folks, but we

knew the adobe worked better. Beaugival was always practical. The house stood on a small hill, and he could see it (and his darling wife inside) from where he worked. The clay color of the house contrasted with the green of the cactuses, the bluish hue of the maguey plants, with the red of the brick garden walls and with an array of potted flowers. At night, these walls were aglow with the lights that flickered from the windows that looked out onto the gardens. When the moon was full, silvery or red, your father and I would take the whole family out to see the Beaugival house, and to listen to La Beaugival play the piano and sing their favorite songs. We didn't know what they meant, but they sounded beautiful:

Au bois de Saint-Cloud
Il y a de petites fleurs,
Il y a de petites fleurs,
Au bois de mon cœur,
Au bois de mon cœur.

There was no doubt that Beaugival and his wife nurtured a loving relationship. He always spoke of her, of her smile, of her long hair, and he never stopped bringing her little gifts. In a sense, their marriage was like the cactuses and the maguey plants that grew strong, lasting for over a hundred years. And we, in turn, were like an extension of their gardens. New growth was always sprouting up here and there, and we cared for them, asking God that they too would live for a hundred years. No one knew why, but the Beaugivals themselves never had any children. And how nice it would have been to see a few Beaugivalitos running about and to hear their tender voices echoing from the Gardens of Versailles.

Though it was just the two of them living in that mansion, every year without fail Beaugival would add another room to the house, which meant coming to hire the Simons boys to work the mud into adobe blocks. One summer your older brother was among the men who were contracted, and it was soon after that he began working for Beaugival on a regular basis. In fact, your brother was the only one that the Beaugivals ever allowed into their secret world. He would carry and position the blocks under the supervision of Beaugival himself. In two weeks they would finish the walls, the windows, the doors, and then Beaugival would show him how to finish the roof with brick tiles. Every so often I'd take lunch to your brother, calling to him from the fence, waiting for the Beaugivals to invite me in, but, not surprisingly, they never did. La Beaugival would take the basket with a "*Merci beaucoup, madame*," and then return to the house as happy as can be, while I just stood there, staring. I wanted so much to know more about her, to be her friend, but she never gave anyone the opportunity.

Just as the house grew with more and more rooms, so too did the stories about the Beaugival property. The neighbors would come over every night to talk to your brother, to ask him to describe what he saw in the ornate rooms of the house and in the Gardens of Versailles. So many people would cram into our little home that those who arrived late found themselves listening from outside the front door. This is how your brother learned to build houses, do roof construction and, of course, tell stories. I remember that your father would get so upset when everyone arrived at once:

"Just how much gossip can the boy have to tell?"

And he would leave your brother to the eager crowd that filled every corner of the house. It was Beaugival and your father who provided your brother with both the knowledge and the financial means to establish his construction company. From the day he began working with Beaugival, your brother would be the only one trusted with their many renovations.

"Now bring me a glass of water, son. My throat is getting dry, and my lips are going numb from all this storytelling."

Beaugival was a scribe. He had a typewriter and an assortment of wooden boxes filled with pens, ink jars, pencils, erasers, rulers and so forth. People would go to him to write letters to their families in Mexico or to a boyfriend or a girlfriend. He also prepared legal documents for the Montebello City Council and for the L.A. Police Department. Beaugival earned his living with a pen and an old typewriter. Every Friday and Saturday he would bring his equipment over and set it up at the Simons store to receive clients. On weekdays, Beaugival was an accountant. He did taxes and prepared contracts that involved large sums of money. They said that he knew about every kind of legal transaction, and that he was a lawyer, though he never identified himself as one. In Simons we all liked him. He was definitely unusual, but he won our trust. Whenever anyone had a problem they came to see your father first and then, if necessary, they would go see Beaugival.

It was on one of these Fridays that Beaugival didn't show up at his usual spot at the Simons store. This would have been back in the 1940s. We thought he was sick because he had also missed the previous Saturday. When he finally did appear, he was smiling in a new Ford that gleamed in the afternoon sun. Stopping by our house he explained that he now worked for the Montebello City Council, and if we needed his services we could find him at City Hall.

"I'll be waiting for you there," he said as he drove off.

And so it happened that a few of us from Simons found our way to City Hall, while others knew better. Many of those who did make the trip to see Beaugival at his new office felt that they had been mistreated or insulted by his secretary. Her name was Mrs. Guajollot. She had a stern face, bad manners and, so they say, the body of a large turkey. Accordingly, the kids came up with her nickname: "La Guajolote," the turkey lady. Beaugival soon realized that it worked best to intercept his Simons neighbors before their encounter with La Guajolote. He would greet us by cheerfully inviting us into his office, and then he'd send her to get coffee and refreshments. With a grim expression she'd comply, returning with a serving tray and a look that betrayed her pronounced indignation toward Mexicans. She would place the tray on the table, turn on her heel and go off in a huff murmuring her usual fire and brimstone. It wasn't long before her notoriety spread throughout Simons. Everyone knew about the turkey lady.

"Watch out for La Guajolote," Beaugival would say laughingly to those contemplating a trip to his office.

Beaugival had been working at City Hall for a number of years when they asked him to take on, as part of his administrative duties, the founding of a library at Simons. He was elated, and he made sure to stop by Simons to announce the news, impressing upon everyone that the proposed library would be a source of great pride for us all. That same day he sought out your brother to discuss the possibility of offering him the building contract. When Beaugival arrived home that night he was in high spirits. He asked his wife to sing in celebration of their good fortune:

Quand il me prend dans ses bras,
Il me parle tout bas
De voir la vie en rose . . .

Over the years Beaugival added more rooms and did more renovations to the house to the point that theirs was the most talked about home in all of Montebello. The Gringos called it "The Beaugival Estates," or "The Beaugival Ranch," or "The Beaugival Hacienda." Visitors would often come to see the so-called hacienda for themselves. Beaugival would host small parties for special guests sent by the mayor to show off Montebello's Spanish-French heritage. The tour would conclude in the Gardens of Versailles, where everyone enjoyed French wines and a performance by La Beaugival.

"After all, isn't Montebello carved on the Arc de Triomphe in Paris?" the mayor would say every time he invited a group to the Beaugival house.

"And our thanks go out to Mr. and Mrs., or Don and Doña, Monsieur and Madame Beaugival: generous people, and a wonderful example of our city's Spanish-French heritage," he would add. As for us Mexicans from Simons, we were never given a second thought. We didn't exist. We didn't belong to Montebello's proud Spanish-French heritage.

The Beaugivals were famous. People from all over would buy tickets at City Hall to visit the Gardens of Versailles and the Beaugival Estates. Ultimately it became Beaugival's new responsibility to serve as a good example of Spanish-French heritage, by receiving guests on a daily basis. La Beaugival played the piano and sang French melodies while lunch or dinner was served in the Gardens of Versailles, followed by drinks in the Beaugival palace room:

Le chant plait à mon âme.
La danse est pour moi
Presque aussi douce qu'un baiser.

Those who had the pleasure of receiving the lavish attention that came with a tour spoke at length of the cultural wonders and of the generosity of the hosts. But not one of us, the people from Simons who had produced the adobe with our bare hands to build the house, had ever stepped inside. Only your older brother could speak firsthand of the wonderment of beholding such luxuries.

The Beaugivals would have been happy to spend the rest of their lives this way, and it must have seemed to them that they would. But in the course of a few days, things changed most unexpectedly. As La Beaugival sat at the piano, two men arrived who walked around the entire property scrutinizing the house.

"Nice place," one of them said at the door as he handed her a card that read "Southern California Edison Company."

"Let's see, how about a little wine before I continue with this story. A little wine always helps me remember the details. Thank you, son."

Shortly thereafter, Beaugival received a letter from the Montebello City Council explaining that the city was interested in their property. It was his understanding that they wanted to establish the Beaugival Estates as a historic site for the State of California. This was great news. He explained to La Beaugival that a contract from the state would provide many benefits for when they retired and, more importantly, it would ensure the preservation of their house and gardens. As always, Beaugival made the rounds at Simons telling his friends that finally the State of California was going to recognize the importance of their heritage in the history of the region. Their house was going to be the monument, the very house that we had helped to build. We shared their enthusiasm and, that night, a few of us went over in the hopes of hearing La Beaugival:

> *La petite Marguerite est tombée*
> *Singulière du bréviaire de l'abbé . . .*

Her songs were so beautiful. And we were truly happy for them both. For the Beaugivals, it must have seemed like a dream come true.

It had all happened so fast. He received the letter on Friday, and they spent Saturday and Sunday celebrating the news. As far as I'm concerned, good news never comes on a weekend and, as it turned out, this was also the case for Beaugival. On the following Monday when he was working in his office, the mayor dropped in and asked:

"So, did you get the letter?"

Beaugival was so absorbed in his work, filling out documents and book acquisitions for the Simons library, that he missed the question entirely. He just stared blankly at the mayor, his thoughts still immersed in the endless volumes of possibility.

"The letter the city sent you?" the mayor repeated impatiently.

"Ah, yes. I understand the city is interested in our estates for a historical monument," Beaugival said cheerfully, his attention still on his work.

"Historical monument?" the mayor looked confused. "Mr. Beaugival, the city wants to rent your land to the Edison Company to put in an electrical substation . . . you know, to benefit all the good people of Montebello."

There was an awkward pause as Beaugival grappled with what he had just heard. Then, searching for his words, he muttered under his breath:

"What? . . . But, what do you mean? What about the house . . . the gardens?"

In his mind's eye he tried to imagine gray, nondescript buildings in the place of their palatial home and magnificent Gardens of Versailles. La Beaugival would rather die than lose all that they had built.

"I don't know what they will do with the house, but the gardens will be bulldozed. Probably the house, too. You see, your property is very valuable. It has direct access to the railroad, the trains, and it borders the river. Don't worry, you'll get a good price for it," the mayor concluded, oblivious to the enormity of his words.

As the mayor went on his way, Beaugival remained motionless, lost in thought.

"There must be some mistake," he told himself. "There had to be a mistake or at least a solution. The City of Montebello can't just take our house from us, our gardens, our property . . . especially after we allowed them to use it as an example of Montebello's Spanish-French heritage. Surely the heritage that they have so often flaunted must be of sufficient value to warrant saving the Gardens of Versailles."

After the initial shock of the news, La Beaugival joined her husband in planning a decisive response to the challenge before them. On the very next day, and at the risk of losing his job, Beaugival approached the city council searching for answers. But each member told him the same thing: that they didn't know, that they hadn't heard anything about such a project, that the city reserved the right to declare "eminent domain" (the public authority to appropriate his land), and that he, Beaugival, would have no legal recourse to protect himself against the loss of the house and gardens. For two days he pursued the matter, and then he received another letter which spelled out in technical terms and legal jargon that indeed the process of eminent domain would be applied to his property, and that he and his wife would have to vacate within a week. This time the Beaugivals announced that they had no intention of leaving, and that city officials would have to remove their dead bodies before they would abandon the home that they loved as much as life itself.

That afternoon your grandmother, Concha, and I had gone to the river looking for one of the herbs that she always picked, and we passed by the Beaugival house. La Beaugival was singing, but her song was cheerless, and I perceived what I thought was a hint of a farewell in her tone:

Méfiez-vous des Blancs, habitants du rivage,
Les Blancs promirent, et cependant
Ils faisaient des retranchements.

The Beaugivals went to ask the mayor, to beg him, to spare the house. But the mayor, accompanied by his wife, replied: "Why do you insist so much? Why do you fight for an old Mexican house that really has no historic value? It's a house made of mud that any greaser could have built."

His wife then added: "Please take the money the city is offering. It's enough to buy a new house near us, where you belong. Take the money, and be happy."

The mayor and his wife showed the Beaugivals the door with forced smiles.

"My son. Do forgive me for going on like this. Should I stop now? Well, bring me another little glass of water. Thank you, son. Now light these candles. It's getting dark."

With primitive machetes they began to hack down the Gardens of Versailles. It was interesting to see how the Edison Company workers entered the gardens. With an enormous tractor they first unearthed a few maguey plants and knocked down a part of the wall, without damaging the house where the Beaugivals had locked themselves in. They just watched from the windows, witnessing how, section by section, the tractors bulldozed and mashed the natural barriers of vegetation, then the brick wall and the wooden fences interlaced with grapevines, rose bushes and bougainvilleas. The vegetable patch, the flower gardens, everything fell before their eyes and, little by little, one foot at a time, the tractors drew nearer the house.

It took the machines barely three days to rub out what had taken years of painstaking labor to build and cultivate. But they avoided the house as the Beaugivals refused to leave. More tractors arrived, along with construction workers. They dug out deep trenches and laid cables and copper tubing. They began installing the guts of the transformers and generators, but still they stayed away from the house.

Two weeks went by, and the Beaugivals stood their ground. When they appeared at the window people from Simons would call out to them, offering them something to eat or drink. But the Beaugivals, instead of responding to our pleas, would return to their piano, and sing.

The mayor came with his wife, as did the director of the Edison Company, and they even asked me to try to convince them to vacate the house. But the Beaugivals remained silent. We were beginning to wonder how they managed without food or water. Finally the Montebello police force and fire department were brought in. They spoke with the company directors who, in the end, decided not to proceed with an arrest.

"Let 'em stay in there until the house falls on top of them for all I care. We're not responsible," one of them decided.

The engineers continued with the construction of the transfer station. They installed the generators, transformers and an array of electrical gadgetry on top of massive cement blocks.

Finally the night came when they announced that they were going to bulldoze the house early the next day. The Beaugivals were required to evacuate by seven in the morning. The news circulated throughout the City of Montebello and Simons.

We, their neighbors from Simons, gathered around seven o'clock at night on the eve of the demolition to plead with the Beaugivals.

"Plácido, please, get out of the house! Plácido, save your wife!" We begged them to put their challenge to rest.

"Non!, nous n'abandonnons jamais notre maison! Merci, nous allons bien, nous n'avons pas peur! Allez-vous-en! Partez!" La Beaugival yelled back at us. No one knew French, but we all understood.

We settled down along the river banks and waited. From a distance we contemplated the house, which was now dwarfed by the enormous steel installations that occupied the space where the gardens once flourished.

By about nine o'clock most people had decided to go home. By midnight only three of us stood watch. An hour later the other two wandered off. Though it was unsettling to find myself alone late at night, I stayed to watch over the house where the Beaugivals awaited their fate.

I kept my vigil on a night when the sky was clear, displaying a divine sea of radiant stars. It was a magical night, weird and wonderful. Then, all at once I heard a crackling sound that came from one of the transformers. This was followed by sparks and more electrical crackling. I stood up and was about to approach the house when a sudden explosion of a thousand volts roared through the air. Sparks and rays of light touched the sky. A strange glow lit up the space where the Gardens of Versailles had once stood and, in an instant, the house turned incandescent with flashes of red, yellow and orange. Everything was ablaze: the house, the Edison building, the steel installations. It all burned in an electric fiery cloud of natural forces.

By daybreak the thundering noise and the pillars of smoke had attracted the entire population of Simons. City officials, the company directors and people from all over Montebello converged on the site to witness the disappearance of the Edison constructions and the Beaugival Estates.

What happened to the Beaugivals themselves remains a mystery. Perhaps they had escaped the explosion and fled before the fire. I don't know. I watched the calamity from beginning to end, and the only thing that I saw was a curtain of sparkling lights rising up into the air.

Curiously enough, after the fire, the Edison Company cancelled the whole project, stating that it wasn't worth it to reconstruct the buildings. For quite some time the land lay vacant. The Beaugival property, the house and the Gardens of Versailles had been all but forgotten until, one day, a gentleman and his family purchased the land. Amid thousands of cactuses and maguey plants tangled with bougainvillea, they built an adobe house that was almost identical to the original. For two years they lived there peacefully when, out of the blue, they vanished without a word to anyone. This started rumors that the property and the house were haunted.

To this day, the property remains a source of unusual energy, a mysterious space where strange things happen. No one dares walk across this land. They say that, at night, far above the cactuses, maguey plants and the abandoned house, you can see two illuminated figures dancing and singing an invitation into the Gardens of Versailles.

"*Though energy goes through continuous transformations, my son, it is never ending. Now, my little curious one, join me for another glass of wine.*"

Author's note:

In December of 1995, my friend Steve Simonian, chief of the Montebello police force, called the university to invite me to see some subterranean rooms that were discovered underneath an old adobe house on Bluff Road. The house had been occupied by many residents who, one after the other, abandoned it after only a few months, claiming that it was haunted.

It was eleven in the morning when I met up with Steve and a few local police and federal officers. We entered the house and descended to a series of ancient catacombs. In one of the rooms there were stockpiles of canned food, various jars and bottles of water. "What I really want you to see is in this last room," Steve said.

On a Mexican blanket, there were two skeletons lying in a close embrace . . .

Prickles

*The labours of men of genius, however erroneously
directed, scarcely ever fail in ultimately turning
to the solid advantage of mankind.*
—Mary Wollstonecraft Shelley

I sat down with my mother in our usual spot in the lush garden.
Her flowers were in full bloom: roses, poppies, carnations,
azaleas and countless other varieties. We sat facing each other
under the cool shade of the old avocado tree. Its robust branches now scraped against the garage of the adobe house that, fifty
years earlier, my father had built from his gambling winnings.
My mother and I sat motionless for half an hour, absorbed in the
freshness and the silence that, in addition to its fruit, the
immense tree provided us over the years.

Stumpy emerged from the neighbor's yard, lumbering
through the hydrangeas. He was an old dog born with one front
leg shorter than the rest. We watched him limp over to his water
dish under the shade of the tree. He had a drink, then came over
to stretch out at my mother's feet. After licking at his paws, he
closed his eyes and drifted into a peaceful sleep. Stumpy also
had his usual spot, just in front of Mom, who nudged him affectionately with her foot. Stumpy lazily opened one eye, resettled
himself and went back to sleep. Now you could see the callused
stump of his bad leg.

I broke the silence: "Remember, Mom, that you were going to tell me more about that famous artist, 'Prickles,' who had lived in Simons?"

"Look at Stumpy, how comfortable he is. Lucky old mutt," was my mother's only reply.

The dog stretched out his legs indulgently and dozed back to sleep. Mom, as if to mimic her favorite animal, straightened her legs and settled herself back in her chair. From where we were sitting you could see the skyscrapers in downtown Los Angeles. The sun was setting behind them, beyond the beaches of Santa Monica. It was October, four days before my birthday, and it was scorching hot. The temperature had risen to almost a hundred degrees, but, mercifully, the tree sheltered us with a delightful freshness.

🐜 🐜 🐜

Prickles lived with his mother on Maple St. until he left for university. She was very young. Her name was Gloria, but the kids started teasing her and nicknamed her "La Glorieta." She was about fifteen or sixteen when she had David, her only child. Gloria gave birth all by herself, without anyone's help. She was so slender that no one realized that she was even pregnant. It came as a real surprise to everyone when, one day, she went out shopping at the Núñez store, carrying a little bundle of joy.

They called David's father "Ol' Caray." No one knew his first name, or his last name for that matter. What people did know was that he was a man of few words. He hardly ever said anything. It was as if he made an effort to never speak. He was twenty-five years older than Gloria. They say that when she had David, Ol' Caray was over forty years old.

Ol' Caray was thin, fair-skinned, with surprisingly thick and shiny black hair. He combed it back like the movie stars. He wasn't very tall, but he was good looking. He had a really nice car that was so clean it shined. He always arrived home carrying brown paper bags and what looked like little gifts for Gloria. Every day, except Fridays, he went into Los Angeles. They say that he worked in Hollywood as an auctioneer; the one who calls out the prices. There were also rumors that he made a lot of money and that he came from a rich family. These kinds of rumors were common in Simons.

Deciding to move in together, Gloria and Ol' Caray rented one of Don Presciliano's houses, the one he had on Maple St. They lived there as a couple for a few years, but they kept their distance from their neighbors in Simons.

Gloria's house was very neat and tidy. From the outside it was nothing special, just like all the other houses on Maple St., but inside she had some of the finest woven oriental rugs you could ever imagine. Every room looked like it had been arranged by one of those interior decorators. And everywhere you looked there were mounds of beautiful quilts. In the back of the house they had added a spacious room where they stored even more quilts, dozens of them, made from precious silk, linen, fine cottons, different fabrics with a variety of textures and colors. She kept the materials in brown paper bags, the same ones that Ol' Caray brought home every day.

That's what she did for work. She made beautiful quilts. She had quilted about a thousand of them, and Ol' Caray sold them in town for a considerable profit. However, she never saw one penny from the money he made. Ol' Caray was obviously exploiting the young girl, forcing her to work hard every day so that he could get rich.

Over time, Ol' Caray began staying in town, not coming home for two, sometimes three days at a time. He told Gloria that he had landed a job with the best auction house in the world, and that he had rented a small apartment near the company headquarters in Santa Monica. The company was called Sotheby's. Ol' Caray promised her that in a year's time he would rent a bigger apartment for the both of them, and then she could go with him. After a while, he only came home a few days a month. And, when he returned to Santa Monica he would take dozens of quilts with him. The day came when he arrived in a brand new pickup truck and filled it with quilts. Poor Gloria just quilted more, sometimes until late at night. She did this because she dreamed of living with Ol' Caray in Santa Monica, in a nice apartment near the beach. There she would be happy with the man she loved with her heart and soul. It was both Gloria's good and bad fortune to have a pure heart and an attractive body.

Ol' Caray's visits became fewer and fewer. He would come to stay the night, and then at daybreak he would leave with a truckload of valuable quilts. Then one day she walked into the Núñez store with her beautiful baby boy.

"How proud his daddy must be!" Mr. Núñez said.

"I wouldn't know. Ol' Caray hardly ever comes around anymore. Now he sends his employees for the quilts."

As for David, he grew up to become quite the little gentleman. He was very cute and very clever. Gloria did everything she could to prepare him for school. At least in this Ol' Caray helped out by bringing David books, paper and pens. Gloria had taught him good manners and how to show respect for his neighbors. David would always say hello whenever he saw other adults. Gloria also began to teach him how to quilt. By the age of four, David could already make some remarkable little quilts. Ol' Caray would take David's quilts as well.

By this time Ol' Caray had practically abandoned his family. He never publicly acknowledged David as his son or Gloria as his wife. And Gloria never countered with any legal action, and she never called him David's father. Nevertheless, Ol'

Caray sent them money, and every two weeks he collected the quilts that Gloria and David made.

David was growing up to be a handsome lad. Gloria loved to dress him in shorts, white shirt and tie, and a jacket. By the age of five, David was clearly the neighborhood favorite. He was only five but he spoke as if he were fifteen. As a young child he possessed a greater vocabulary than some adults. He was a real wonder.

He made friends with kids from all over the neighborhood. All the moms wanted their kids to play with David so they would learn his good manners and how to read and write.

On his first day of school David, holding on to Gloria's hand, and dressed in his usual shorts, jacket and tie, led a whole procession of little kids, their mothers and a few neighbors. They all entered the kindergarten room, and the teacher, Mrs. Miranda, the only teacher in the whole school that spoke Spanish, seated the children on a big rug in the middle of the room. But before Mrs. Miranda could get started, David stood up to say that he had something for her and for each of his classmates.

Gloria placed two big bags in front of David. He opened one of them, taking out a beautiful quilt, and he laid it in Teacher Miranda's arms. She just stood there staring at the quilt, stunned by its beauty. Meanwhile, David and Gloria handed out quilts to all the other children who were starting school. Those quilts soon became prized possessions. All the kids would snuggle up with one come nap time.

Ol' Caray came by a few days later, and when he found out that they had given away so many quilts, he became furious, yelling that he didn't support them just so they could give away his merchandise to all the neighborhood riffraff. Ol' Caray's screaming could be heard all the way to the Núñez store, where a few women happened to be gathered. They quickly agreed to go help her, and by the time they arrived, there were about ten of them to confront Ol' Caray who had begun loading his pick-up with armfuls of quilts.

"Not those ones! Those belong to me!" shouted Gloria, who ripped them from his arms.

He grabbed her by the hair and, just as he was about to slap her, the throng of women threw themselves on him with brooms, sticks and quilts. Ol' Caray jumped into his truck. But before he got away, the women managed to get all the quilts back.

Gloria met his gaze for the last time and shouted very deliberate words at him: "Beat it, you loser! I don't ever want to see your face again! We don't need you for anything! And, just so you know, you're not David's father, so go to hell, you dumb-ass prick!"

Ol' Caray was stunned. He looked over at David, who stood beside his mother. Roaring his engine, he then took off down Maple St., as the kids all say, "burnin' rubber."

The thing is that Gloria, after a few months, found herself needing a job. With the Christmas season drawing near, she figured that she could sell a few quilts on her own. And so they went to speak with Mr. Núñez to ask his permission to sell quilts at his store. To Gloria's relief, he agreed, on the condition that David spend a few hours helping out at the store on Saturdays and Sundays. Mr. Núñez was also very fond of David. The idea of selling quilts at Mr. Núñez's store was a big success. But what attracted people even more was David himself. People came from all around to see him, to speak with him and to buy his quilts.

Throughout the whole Christmas season, Gloria and David worked very hard, and they sold many quilts, which had become quite fashionable. It wasn't long before a few furniture shop managers approached Gloria to request that she make some quilts for them. She said that she would, provided that they supply the materials, pay her a salary and include medical insurance. She wasn't prepared to work on commission. It happened that as many as five different furniture factories accepted her terms. Three of these factories—Bucarines on Rodeo, Etan and Banks—were big businesses that operated out of Beverly Hills, Brentwood and Santa Monica, where Ol' Caray worked.

Soon after, Gloria barged into the Núñez store wound up about something, crying hysterically. She had David by the hand. He seemed half scared to death. Mr. Núñez gave him a candy, but he burst into tears from the fright his mother was giving him. When finally he fell asleep on the lazy-boy behind the counter, Mr. Núñez approached Gloria.

"For God's sake, woman, what's wrong? What happened?"

Gloria pulled him over to David. She lifted David's arm and turned it to show his elbow.

"Look at that! Can't you see?"

"See what, Gloria?"

"Look at that thing, the bone that's coming out of his elbow!"

Mr. Núñez looked more closely at his elbow. He touched it and compared it to the other. Gloria was right. He had some kind of growth that felt like a bone, growing out of his elbow. The thing had a tip to it.

Then, Gloria lifted his shirt.

"Look!" she said. "Look what's happened to my David."

Unable to contain herself, she fell to her knees crying.

David had a dozen of these hard, pointy things growing on his ribs. They grew directly from the bone, stretching the young boy's skin. His chest was covered with them. They didn't seem to be hurting him any. There were more on his back, but still none on his legs or around his head.

Very early the next day, Gloria, David and Mr. Núñez went to see the doctor at Simons. Dr. Walland was the only one that folks trusted. He knew the Simons people well and, when necessary, he would even make house calls. He knew everyone, and he helped deliver many Simons children. He was a truly generous man.

They arrived at his office at eight o'clock sharp and entered as a group. There were already patients in the waiting room. There was no receptionist or nurse. Dr. Walland took care of everything himself without any help. They sat down, except for David who stood at his mother's side. When David realized that the other patients were looking at him strangely, he hid his face in his mother's lap. At that moment Gloria couldn't help the flood of tears that poured out of her for beautiful David. She held him tightly against her bosom and covered his face with kisses. David started laughing from all the ticklish kisses.

Dr. Walland asked them into his office. Smiling, he calmly examined David, who talked about his school and his friends. He told David that he needed to take some blood. David offered his left arm and didn't so much as flinch from the needle.

David spent the next couple of weeks at home. The doctor wanted to make sure that whatever David had wasn't contagious. But he was unable to identify the illness. David's disorder was extremely rare, of that he was certain.

Then a series of examinations began at the hands of various specialists at the White Memorial Hospital, where they had a research center for rare diseases. They explained to Gloria that they didn't know how many more tumors might grow, nor could they predict the consequences should the tumors begin growing on the inside. It seemed that, for now, they only grew outward. After almost a month of studies, they found neither the cause nor the cure for David's tumors. On the last day they examined him, he was discharged without any medication, just a card indicating that he needed to return in a month's time.

Gloria and David never did return to the hospital. They carried on with their lives in the little house that she had bought on Maple St. They never expelled David from school, even though he had a gruesome condition. If anything, his illness drew the children even closer to him. They protected him, and some even helped him with his quilting. It was thanks to the quilts that mother and child could make a living.

Though the tumors never ceased to sprout from David's bones, it seemed that he and his mother got on with life pretty well. She was making and selling more quilts than ever before. And then it happened that the quilts that David made began to increase in value. The people that came for the quilts, and they came from everywhere, saw David and considered him a phenomenon, and then they wanted to buy the quilts made specifically by him. The day came when he was so popular that he took special orders for quilts. And he charged a handsome fee for these.

David was about twelve when he left elementary school for junior high. He breezed through school. He learned quickly and retained what he learned. Gloria bragged about his excellent grades, straight As. But then one day after school, while waiting for the bus, David found himself surrounded by three boys from ninth grade. They started poking at the tumors on his face and arms, asking him if he was a leper. They told him that soon he was going to go crazy and die. They said things that were really cruel. They pushed him around and forced him to the back of the line.

David's friends tried to defend him, but the boys were too big and they started to bully them as well. David's defenders retreated only to see the boys rough him up even more. Though he knew that he was on his own, David wouldn't bow down. The biggest boy punched him in the mouth, cutting his lip open. When the bus arrived, the driver got out to help David off the ground and into the bus. For the whole drive home David's attackers teased him. They all laughed at his tumors. They made fun of his face, his deformed head, his bumpy hands and the loose shirt and pants that he wore.

That was the day that David's endless suffering began. His tumors appeared to grow larger and pointier, especially the ones on his head and face. The ones on his feet caused him so much pain when he walked that Gloria had to make him special slippers with quilted soles. David began to walk as if his feet were on fire, and so the boys made fun of him even more. One day at school they surrounded him again. Denny, the toughest boy in the group, planted himself face-to-face with David.

"You horny toad monster, you gross me out!" God knows how many insults he yelled at him. David tried to punch him, but he missed, falling next to a big cactus that grew in the middle of the schoolyard. Denny laughed and yelled at him.

"Get up, cactus face! You heard me, Prickles. Get on your feet!"

David got up and managed to grab hold of Denny and land a few punches with his tumored fists. Then he head butted Denny so hard that he knocked him unconscious.

A teacher arrived on the scene and separated them. He took David to the principal's office. From inside the building he could hear the gang of kids yelling, "Prickles knocked out Denny! Prickles kicked Denny's ass!"

From that day on, everyone called David "Prickles."

Gloria and David went through a period of crisis. All at once, from one day to the next, it was as if Gloria had lost her mind. She started dressing provocatively, wearing miniskirts and low-cut blouses. She went out with various men who took her out dancing in Hollywood. The neighbors said that, when her dates took her home, these men would kiss and grope her. She would go into the Núñez store with David's quilts and come out with bottles of white wine. She waited for her dates outside her house, while drinking from a bottle of wine.

One afternoon after David got home from school, he heard strange noises coming from his mother's bedroom. Putting his ear to the door, he could hear moans and whispering between Gloria and some stranger, who were in the throes of passion. He slowly opened the door to peek in at what his mother was doing. The scream that he let out was so startling that it made the two lovers jump right out of bed. Kicking and punching wildly, David threw himself onto the intruder, who still bears the scar on his face.

Gloria suffered the humiliation of being caught in the act. Her son had seen her naked in bed with a man, and it took her months before she would recuperate from the fear of his abnormal, unearthly scream. Mother and son fought all night long. They awoke the next morning still blaming each other for their misery. It was then that David confessed to his mother that he felt a strong attraction to some of the girls at school. But because of his illness he knew that he would not be able to come near them, never love, touch or kiss a pretty girl.

"I'm a sick monster!" he cried, collapsing at his mother's feet. "Why am I even alive?"

Desperate to ease her son's pain, she hugged him, kissed him and begged his forgiveness. And from that moment, she dedicated her life to David. Gloria did everything for him. She took him out of the public system and put him in a Catholic high school. This particular one was well-known for its challenging curriculum and its acceptance of only the most promising students. Gloria took her son to write a series of exams. He passed them with such high scores that they considered him a genius and immediately offered him a scholarship. It had a lasting effect on David's self-esteem to be called a genius. And he deserved it, too, because no one around Simons ever stood out in school. By comparison, his old schoolmates were as sharp as a sack of hammers. But David, he was special. And he knew it.

David finished high school and was accepted at a prestigious private university. Once the other students got used to David, he became very popular. His room was always piled high with quilts, and he began showing his friends how he made them. He even became friends with some very pretty girls. One of them was named Melissa, and it didn't take long for David to fall in love with her. He wanted to get close to her, but, aware of his physical condition, he considered himself lucky just to be her friend. When he used to come home for the summer, he would get all wound up to see her again. Gloria encouraged David to invite her over, but he told her that he was too embarrassed to invite her to their house in such a neighborhood. Melissa was a rich girl who would no doubt feel sorry for the way that he lived. David started calling her on the phone, though, spending hours talking with her. They were in touch so often that eventually even Gloria and Melissa's mother got to know one another, and they decided that they themselves should meet. Melissa's mother came to Los Angeles to visit a relative in Pasadena, and that's where Gloria and Mrs. Dierdock first met. She and Gloria talked about what had been going on between David and Melissa. Then the day came when Gloria invited Melissa's mother to visit. Mrs. Dierdock just loved all the quilts that Gloria and David had made, and she wanted to talk to Gloria about the possibility of taking on special orders as gifts for her employees and clients. Gloria didn't tell any of this to David, who had returned to university for his third year. By this time, David and Melissa had become very close friends. She confessed her most personal problems and feelings to him, and he shared some of his private concerns as well, without ever revealing his true feelings for her, as he sank deeper and deeper into the abyss of unrequited love.

David's love for Melissa filled his life with physical and psychological torture. To see her every day and not caress her, hug her or kiss her passionately made him feel even more abnormal. Sometimes his tumors came out more suddenly and were more pointy and painful than usual. But David suffered his condition in silence, resigned to be just friends with the girl he adored, the girl for whom he would give his life. He told her this more than once. One time he even had to come to her defense against some football players. It was at a party. Stanford had just beaten UCLA, meaning a trip to the Rose Bowl, and one of the football players, Craig, started coming on to Melissa to the point where she had to ask him to leave her alone. But he persisted, and she was forced to push him away. When Craig tried to grab hold of her, David stepped in.

"If you touch her, you'll have to deal with me!"

When this young jock heard David's threat, he broke away laughing, and replied, "Okay, I give up, thorn face. You're too scary for me. I wouldn't want to get poked by one of your stingers!"

By this time everyone was laughing.

"Or get scratched by one of his prickers!" a teammate called out.

They all laughed at David, as he hobbled out of the house with Melissa by his side.

That's how David lived out his third and fourth years at the university, with the impossibility of love standing before him every day. To distract himself from his frustration, David quilted, and he began to paint. He took every painting course that the university had to offer. And he demonstrated such a talent that his professors recommended that he continue studying at a private school. David fit right in. His sensitivity was such that when they showed him a piece by a famous artist, by studying the colors, brushstrokes and texture, he could identify with the artist's emotional state. He would agonize over the suffering or rejoice in the artist's ecstasy. David could reproduce the painting as if the artist had been resurrected to paint it himself. A number of Stanford researchers, art professors and psychologists began to take a serious interest in David. He produced paintings depicting scenes from his own life: his childhood, his parents, the neighborhood, whatever he could remember. Many of these were like photographs. He also did abstract paintings, strange pieces that no one understood, except the art critics, who deemed them to be extraordinary. Melissa was the one who encouraged him the most. She collected all of his paintings. The day came when he sold one of them, not because he was trying to, but, rather, because a couple from Palo Alto just wouldn't take no for an answer. They loved that painting so much.

"The painting is family, happy family, and that's us. What do you want for it?"

"I don't want to sell it," David replied.

"Please, Mr. David," their little girl pleaded with him.

"Five hundred for the painting," the father offered.

"Five hundred? Fine, if it makes you happy."

When more people came in search of David's paintings, Mrs. Dierdock proposed that Melissa and Gloria open up a small gallery in Palo Alto. They could sell David's paintings and his quilts, Gloria's too.

The inauguration attracted a great deal of attention. All of David's friends were in attendance to celebrate his success as a painter and quilter. And, much to their surprise, even Craig appeared, albeit awkwardly, in atonement perhaps for the confrontation that weighed heavy on his conscience. Also present were the usual university brass, various professors, art enthusiasts and the press. David stood in the middle of them all, with

Melissa at his side. She would be his manager and accountant. Behind them, their mothers watched on.

David and Gloria carried on with their new business, and they did very well. David started earning money, and more and more acclaim. But even this newfound success could not satisfy his longing for Melissa. He yearned for her. He dreamed of holding her, of caressing her skin, of sleeping wrapped in her body. To take her in his arms for just the briefest moment would have given him some reprieve from his burning desire, but this would never come to pass. To Melissa, David had become a friend, colleague and brother. "I love you like a brother, you know." With these words, she broke David's heart.

The owner of the premises, a man without any family who very much admired David and Melissa, offered them the building where they had set up the gallery. Melissa was ecstatic. David's thoughts turned immediately to how he could expand his work space. He made plans to convert the top floor into an apartment and studio. He knocked out walls, put in new wiring and plumbing, and installed a kitchen and bathroom. The studio became his own private world where he painted and quilted behind closed doors. No one else was allowed to enter. Not even Melissa was permitted to set foot into his secret space. In this way he took out his revenge against the world, against his sickness, against the new tumors that broke out on his body, against the frustration of loving Melissa, and against Melissa herself who could never love him back.

David worked long hours painting in the studio. In his paintings he captured images of everyday life: workers in the fields, children walking to school, old folks, lovers in the park, Chicano students at Stanford, police officers, gangsters and priests. One such priest, a Chicano, purchased a number of the paintings in which he recognized members of his congregation. These he hung in his church, Iglesia Católica la Purísima.

David was asked to drop off the order himself and, while he was there, the priest presented him with a painting of the Virgin of Guadalupe. Though he would never fully understand the source of his inspiration, David felt compelled to begin a series of his own portrayals of the Virgin. He depicted Her in the daily life of the Chicano community. He picked out the odd painting from this series for sale in the gallery, but he kept most of the others for himself.

What happened next to David was just one of those things that unexpectedly changes one's life forever. He was working away in the room that they used for an office, going over the accounts with Melissa, when a man walked in. Tall with broad shoulders, wearing jeans and a vest over his T-shirt, the man looked at Melissa and said in a gruff voice, "Prickles! Where's Pri . . . Prickles!"

Melissa was startled by his aggressive tone, and she noticed that he staggered like he had had too much to drink. The various patrons made their way to the other end of the gallery, avoiding the man who was apparently drunk. Melissa walked over to the telephone to call the police, but stopped short when she heard him say:

"I'm here to b-buy Prickles' Vir-Virgin paintings."

David emerged to help ward off the vagrant, who sluggishly reiterated his request, searching for his words in the fog of inebriation. When the man saw David, he stumbled over to give him a hug.

"Prickles, you don' remember me. I'm the guy who p-pushed you 'round in grammar school and named you Prickles!"

David recognized him immediately and drew a calm breath. The memory came back vividly of the day they had fought in the schoolyard.

"I wan' t-to see your Virgin pain-paintings. I'm Denny. I'm not here f-for a rematch. I'm here to buy! So sh-show me!"

David had good reasons to be suspicious of him. How was he going to pay for the paintings? He appeared a little down on his luck. Calmly and politely, David showed him a few of the Virgin of Guadalupe paintings. Denny looked them over, disconcerted and perplexed. He frowned and shook his head.

"That's nice! Nice! But they're not y-yours. I wan' your p-paintings."

"They're mine, all of these are mine!" David replied.

"No-no you did-didn't sign them. Who in the 'ell is D-David?"

Melissa returned with two of David's most recent paintings which hadn't yet been signed.

"I'm David."

"No, you-you Prickles. Prickles, and you shou-should be proud of it," Denny said as he grabbed one of the paintings from Melissa and held it up to get a better look.

"I don' like this as much as the oth-others, but I'll, I'll take it. But you must sign, sign 'Prickles.'"

It turned out that Denny had ended up studying computer science and had set up his own company to sell computer parts. His business grew to be a multi-million dollar enterprise, with factories in Santa Ana, Saratoga and Tijuana. He had a house in Saratoga and another in Villa Park, both of them exclusive neighborhoods for the wealthy. Denny bought a fortune's worth of paintings from David, and he sent several other wealthy clients his way to buy even more.

As they loaded one of the Virgin paintings into his truck, Denny explained his own physical condition to David, "P-Polio, a bout with polio. That's why I sha-shake and sp-speak slow. It g-got me when I wa-was fifteen. Doctors said the d-disease had disappeared, bu-but it came back. Everything, everything c-comes back, you know."

🐞 🐞 🐞

Renowned for his paintings and his nickname, Prickles' reputation as an artist grew in both national and international circles. He received several prestigious awards from universities and art institutes. But in spite of this growing fame and fortune, David still felt very much alone in life and empty in his heart. His love for Melissa never waned. If anything, it grew more intense. There were times when he just stared at her and trembled with desire. Then, another unexpected visitor, Craig, showed up one day at the gallery. It was Melissa he was interested in, not the paintings. Before long she was going out with him, the rising football star and, before David's very eyes, the two of them fell in love. They were always together. Whenever David saw Melissa, he knew that Craig wasn't far behind and, if he said hello to Craig, it could only mean that Melissa would be arriving soon. Instead of suffering through the sight of them, David would disappear into his studio and begin breaking open some of the tumors on his body. All bloodied, he endured the agony as a calming distraction from his jealousy.

There were no treatments to improve his condition. Nothing could cure him physically or spiritually, and he suffered this torment alone.

One night, after the gallery was closed and Melissa and Craig had gone out to the movies, David retreated to the seclusion of his studio to resume painting. Sometime after midnight he descended to the gallery in search of some sketches he had been working on. As he came down the stairs he heard Craig and his beloved Melissa whispering in the darkness, and he was heartened at the thought of seeing her just once more that night. But when his eyes adjusted to the darkness, he realized that Melissa was sitting on Craig's lap with her blouse wide open. David froze. He lost his breath at the sight of Craig burying his face between Melissa's breasts, feeling her, savoring her and inhaling her all at the same time. David felt suffocated by the rage that exploded in his thorny head. Retracing his steps, he climbed back to his studio and quietly locked the door. He started rupturing the tumors on his face and body. Then he split open some of the tumors that swelled around his groin, stifling his screams as the blood began to flow once more. He turned on all the lights, then sat there contemplating his self-mutilation. When he was completely undressed, he saw that the hardwood floors were all bloodied. He turned to stare at the Virgin of Guadalupe, who was watching him from the paintings that he had leaned against the wall.

Insolently, David spoke to this pure woman who loves all of God's creatures, "And do you love me lil' Virgin, Mother of Jesus, your Son, another poor bastard who was sacrificed, who couldn't screw any of the women he loved, the women who followed him around secretly hoping for just one chance at ecstasy?"

David threw the paintings to the floor, then grabbed the oil paints, every color within reach, threw them all on the canvases where the Virgin held her gaze. Naked and covered in blood, he squatted down and sat on the Virgin and began to rub his blood into the painting. He turned over onto his stomach and began shoving his penis against Her. In the ooze of the canvas, he felt that She reciprocated, soothing every tumor on his body. David poured more paints onto the sacred images and, burning with passion, he thrust himself against Her repeatedly until the Virgin squeezed all the energy out of his body. His orgasm was so satisfying and complete that it left him shuddering until he finally came to rest in a deep sleep.

The next morning after a long bath, David went to clean up the mess he had made. But as he approached the paintings strewn about the floor, he was taken aback by what he saw. One of the images of the Virgin was completely covered in an abstract configuration of intricately combined colors. The Virgin had disappeared underneath the chaos, leaving David with an extraordinary painting. He could hardly take his eyes off it.

"Virgin lover, thank you for this offering," he gasped.

David signed the painting "Prickles" and took it down to the gallery, where Melissa was busy arranging an exhibit before opening. David, without saying a word, held it up in front of her.

"Oh my God . . . that's beautiful, David. Is this a new style? We have to put it in the window right away. You're amazing, you really are amazing."

"As are you."

"Title?"

"Virginal Gift."

"Are there more?"

"Yes."

"When can you bring them down?"

"It'll take a while . . . to develop this new technique."

Melissa smiled and placed David's latest masterpiece in the front window. It wasn't long before a few who passed by gathered to contemplate the amazing painting.

"People seem to like it, David. What should we price it at?"

"I don't know. What's it worth to you?"

"I think you've broken your high with this one. I'd say ten thousand and see what happens."

At that moment, the door opened and Craig walked in. He looked right at David and said, "That's the coolest painting I've ever seen."

All the fuss was simply too much to bear. David escaped from the gallery through the back door and made his way to the distant hills by the university, searching for the Virgin in the peace and quiet of natural surroundings.

The days passed, and Melissa and Craig continued to arrive after hours to use the gallery's office for their romantic encounters while, in the studio directly above them, the Virgin revealed Herself to David on his canvases. She stretched out Her arms, and David, naked and all covered in paint, pressed his body to Hers, twisting and convulsing. He felt the Virgin burning under his weight, as Melissa, in turn, consumed her lover downstairs. In a way, David felt happy for Craig, and he felt blessed by the Virgin, hearing Her voice inside his head, "Love me with your heart, your body and your soul, devour me with your flesh and blood, become one with me."

David, in a desperate attempt to fulfill Her commands, spread his legs on the Virgin's face, rubbing the paint from his anus and testicles into the image of his Divine Beloved. He contorted his body, tortured by the pain in his tumors as they broke open and bled on the canvas. His blood mixed with the paint as he embraced Her warm body. It lasted for hours until his orgasm culminated in a spiritual communion with the Virgin, who smiled back at him compassionately. As he slept, She appeared to him in a dream, guiding him to an artist's workshop where he saw himself working with three young students.

⁂

David understood the message he had received from the Virgin of his dreams. The very next morning he explained to Melissa that he planned to open up a workshop where he would take on student apprentices. Wasting no time, he made inquiries about renting out the space next door to the gallery, which had been a clothing boutique that had closed after only a few years of operation. Having given up her business, the previous leaseholder decided not to renew her contract. David offered to rent the space for five years, but at half the price. After a few days the owner agreed on the condition that he also be given five of David's paintings, three of which he would pick out right away and the other two to be chosen after the workshop's first year of production. With the contract signed, David had found the perfect space for expansion.

The first of his apprentices was Ronaldo Ocampo, a boy from Stanford who studied chemistry and, in his spare time, painted murals. Next was a high school student, Eduardo Kim, who liked to use human figures in his representation of buildings. Some of the more controversial images that he employed in his paintings had landed him in trouble. Eventually they fired the art teacher who had fostered his unconventional style. The third artist was Rita Deford, an art history student who painted landscapes and urban scenery with superior skill. Convinced by not only the quality of her art, David included her in the workshop because he was also intrigued by Rita's physical condition. She was really tall, with black curly hair, a round face with dimpled cheeks, and a strong body, like a weightlifter's. When he dropped by the university to meet her, David was greeted with the usual alarm that his condition provoked. All was forgiven once the head of the fine arts department arrived to make the introductions. David was escorted to meet the young girl who had applied to "The Prickles Workshop."

"She always works alone," the professor said.

"Why?" asked David.

"Rita is the most talented artist I've ever worked with," was his reply.

"Why does she work alone?" David repeated his question.

"You'll have to see for yourself, then you'll understand."

He and David climbed the stairs to the art studios. Soon they heard the sounds of moans and howling. They crept over to a balcony and peered over. Down below, in the studio hall, a girl was painting with her whole body in motion, but not exactly the way David did. She painted with her right hand, and each movement that she made with the brush was reflected in her left hand, accompanied by bizarre groans. The movements were sometimes smooth and fluid, and other times violent. Rita's emotions were expressed through the left side of her body. Thus, whenever she got excited, each brushstroke triggered a vigorous reflex in her left-side extremities.

From the balcony David watched Rita as she shook and tumbled about the painting that was beginning to take form. The normal rhythm of any other painter was translated by Rita into a succession of twists, turns and physical stuttering, leaving her dripping with sweat. Her enormous effort resulted in a number of intriguing paintings that depicted medieval and gothic religious scenes, in which grotesque figures appeared against a backdrop of natural beauty. Her paintings were an echo of her physical struggle: one side serene and the other violent and distorted.

"Of course Rita knows all about you. And she hopes you'll understand her particular situation," the professor said.

And that's how "The Prickles Workshop" came into being, with Ronaldo Ocampo, Eduardo Kim and Rita Deford as the first apprentices. And, in the first year, on David's insistence, these painters also learned how to quilt. After much training, they eventually produced quilts that the master himself deemed worthy of offering to the public.

The workshop was a success, adding further to the gallery's reputation. Numerous articles were written about David in some of the country's most widely read magazines and academic journals. They talked about David's life, his condition and his artistic prowess. The media exposure attracted even more enthusiasts to his gallery. They wanted to meet, or at least see, "the artist with a thousand horns over his body." People came from around the world to buy his paintings.

One evening they were all eating supper at Melissa's apartment, when the phone rang. It was for David, but he wasn't interested in talking to anyone, so he passed the phone back to Melissa and headed for the door.

"Really? Wow, that's fantastic!" Melissa exclaimed as she began scribbling down notes. When she got off the phone, she turned to look for David, but he had already left. Back in the privacy of his studio, he bid his Beloved Virgin good night, and She held him, pressing his tumored head against Her naked breasts.

The next morning the newspapers in Monterrey and San Francisco ran articles about "the first ever recipient of the MacArthur Fellowship to hail from the Bay Area, a Palo Alto-based artist who . . . " David had reached the pinnacle of artistic achievement by winning America's most prestigious award. Overnight the value of his artwork doubled. A flood of offers came in from museums, art institutes and universities, all wanting to host a visit from Prickles, the genius. But he would reject them all, choosing a life of solitude instead. His daily routine of walking through the local hillsides and painting in the privacy of his studio continued uninterrupted. And, at night, he suckled Her virginal breasts engorged with milk and rubbed his own bodily fluids into Her, mixing blood with paint into a work of art that they produced as one.

By this time, David's secret obsession with Melissa had begun to change. His longing to possess her slowly subsided. He loved her dearly, but he no longer yearned for her body. Instead, it was the Virgin's body that fed both his carnal and spiritual libido. Night after night, She would appear to him on the canvas, only to be transfigured by their sexual union, creating new images, products of divine love. More and more, he craved the Virgin's body.

One quiet afternoon when nothing really mattered except the fresh air, when the autumn wind chilled the last of warm summer days, Melissa, Craig and David were going about their business arranging new paintings in the gallery's front window. A man carrying what appeared to be a painting wrapped in brown paper approached the gallery with two women following behind. They stopped when they saw David. One of the women pointed and, without diverting their impertinent gaze from him, the three held a brief discussion, nodded their agreement and then made their way toward the door. Melissa greeted them politely as they entered, but they did not reply. Instead the man very purposely placed the painting in front of her and began removing the brown paper. Then, trembling slightly, the man said, "We want to speak with the artist, no, the person who painted this."

"It's titled 'Apparition.'" Melissa recognized the painting right away. She looked at the painting, then over at David and said confidently, "One of his best. Here's the artist himself."

"Artist? He's no artist! He's a desecrator of all that is holy. He's a manifestation of the Devil." The man spoke in a loud voice now, for all to hear.

From her purse one of the women took out a small jack-knife. While the other held the painting, the man watched closely and she began scraping away at the outer layer.

"No!" Melissa shrieked. "You're destroying the painting!" She made a move toward the woman, but the man intervened.

"Look at what this abomination of a human being has done!" said the man. He was referring to the figure that appeared from behind the swirl of colors that the woman carefully scraped away. The image of the Virgin of Guadalupe was unmistakable.

"You have defiled one of Christianity's most sacred images!"

He gestured dramatically as the woman continued excavating, excited by the magnitude of the sin she was uncovering.

The man turned his attention to the gallery showroom, motioning to other paintings as he decried in a grave tone, "God's punishment will destroy the Devil's creations! Just how many of these paintings conceal the image of our Sacred Mother. This one? What about this one here?"

While Melissa, Craig and David followed after the man to keep him from touching any of the artwork, the two women grabbed the nearest painting, titled "Virgin Paradise," and began to scrape away with the jackknife.

Upon discovery that it too concealed an image of the Virgin of Guadalupe, one of the women cried out, "My Holy Virgin! What have these demons done to you!"

The other woman turned toward David and proclaimed, "Christ will punish you for damaging his Holy Mother, you deformed abomination. Your evil marketplace will be stoned and destroyed!"

David considered their words calmly while looking at the damaged painting. He concluded that they were just a bunch of fanatics, as Craig and Melissa hurried them toward the door.

"That's fine. You can stone me later," said David, "but now I want you out of my gallery. Get out of here before I call the police."

The confrontation had been unsettling, but they convinced themselves that it had just been the random act of a bunch of sectarian fanatics to whom they should pay no more attention.

Melissa said goodnight to David with a reassuring hug and then a question, "So, why did you paint over the Virgin of Guadalupe?"

"Because She loves me."

When their eyes met, David smiled, then turned to go up to his studio. There, in his secret world, he spent the entire night naked, his body lathered in bright colors, bonding with the Virgin of Guadalupe. That night the Virgin appeared to him nude, young with creamy thighs, firm breasts with dark nipples and long-flowing hair framing Her elegant neck. The Virgin spread Her legs, opening Her clitoris to David. She pulled Her lover's mouth onto Her breast, where he suckled the warm milk that nursed his very soul. It felt so good. And when the pleasure was too much to bear, he surrendered completely to his body. Twisting and turning from the intensity of his orgasm, his tumors broke open against the sperm-covered canvas. Then suddenly he noticed something he hadn't before: a trickle of blood began to flow from his palms, and from the soles of his feet.

Bewildered, he heard the Virgin speak: "Consume me, eat from my body and you will find salvation."

When he awoke the next morning, he discovered that he had completed yet another masterpiece. Triumphantly he brought it down to have it showcased in the front window. By closing time it had sold. In spite of the earlier threats from the religious fanatics, David continued to paint over images of the Virgin of Guadalupe, proudly displaying his abstract creations in the gallery's front window. He was determined not to let anyone interfere with his artistic freedom or, more importantly, his relationship with Her.

🐝 🐝 🐝

David's life settled into a comfortable routine, reflected in the activity that surrounded him. From his studio he watched the birds flutter about the sidewalk, disturbed by whoever passed by, or he lingered in quiet contemplation of the most recent exhibit. He regularly met with his apprentices in the workshop next door, where they discussed their projects with other students and invited guests. Life in Palo Alto, Stanford and its environs was peaceful, with people relatively happy just going about their daily lives. Daybreak in Palo Alto was the same as in any other all-American town.

It was, however, on such a morning that David ran into further trouble. Descending with his latest creation, he cheerfully greeted Melissa, who paused from her accounting duties to admire the painting. Then he proceeded to the front window. He saw the paper boy and a few of the local shopkeepers, but instead of the usual hustle and bustle of morning activity, he sensed an eerie calm. When he finished setting up the painting, he joined Melissa in the office to make himself a cup of coffee. Pensive, David concentrated on the tapping of his spoon against the cup as he stirred in the sugar. Then the morning stillness was broken by a sudden commotion that seemed to erupt out of nowhere. In front of the gallery a crowd of protesters had gathered, carrying signs that denounced David for his desecration of the Virgin of Guadalupe. The protesters had blocked off all traffic. Melissa immediately called the police, but they didn't come right away. Instead, more protesters arrived, adding to the uproar. Melissa called the police again to see what was taking so long but, to her disbelief, they took no notice of her sense of urgency. The crowd attempted to force open the doors, and they banged on the windows with masked images of the Virgin, and with crucifixes made of wood, silver and gold. Others prayed or chanted their devotion to the Virgin. Never before in the history of Palo Alto had such a representative cross-section of the population gathered with a common cause. There were men and women of all ages, and children too. There were urban professionals dressed in suits, landowners and farm workers, students and church ladies. They came from every walk of life to accuse David of blasphemy, to hold him accountable for the unpardonable sin of desecrating the Virgin Mother.

David just stood there watching them as they pressed up against the front window. They were pushing so hard from behind that the masked Virgins appeared deformed against the glass. Like a uterus crammed full of humanity, the window gave way, and God's blessed children spilled in. Seeing a dozen men and women struggling ridiculously in a pile of glass, posters and paintings brought a vengeful smile to David's lips. Still on the phone, Melissa was now screaming at the police station dispatcher.

"They're breaking windows and they're going to kill us!"

Outside, the sound of sirens finally came, followed by the policemen.

David tried in vain to salvage some of the paintings that the raging mob vehemently destroyed. He threw himself on them, ignoring the pain from his tumors. The mob countered David's punches with a flurry of blows that broke open his many wounds. When David fell to the floor, bleeding and convulsing from the intensity of the beating, the mob began kicking him from all sides. He screamed in agony, but they wouldn't stop. Melissa broke away from the men who were holding her back, and she ran to David to shield him with her own body. At that moment, when he saw the face of the woman he so loved grimacing next to his, and in spite of the fists and feet that rained down on him, he felt an unnatural strength surge from within that launched him to his feet.

He roared out at the crowd, "Fuck the Virgin of Guadalupe!"

The rage in his guttural voice stopped the protesters in their tracks who, stunned, looked uneasily at one another. A heavy silence fell over the crowd which, moments later, was interrupted by the policemen who finally made their way through.

That night, the life and times of "Prickles" once again became a matter for international media coverage. From California to New York, from Canada to Mexico, David's illness, his artistic genius and now his sacrilege against the Virgin of Guadalupe and God had earned him an instant of tumored face time on the television screens across the continent. At the monster's side you saw "his beautiful lover." This was the description of Melissa by the TV and radio announcers which was later confirmed in black and white in all the newspapers.

The night of the attack, the ground floor of the gallery, strewn with broken glass and debris, remained open as a crime scene. Curious onlookers strolled past to see where it had all happened, hoping to catch a glimpse of the phenomenon that had painted over the Virgin of Guadalupe. Cars slowed down, the drivers peeking out at the night vigil of a group of fanatics who huddled together to protect the Virgin from further abuse. The police patrols remained behind to urge everyone to continue on their way. As they were leaving, some of the onlookers peered up at the top floor where the sinner or, for some, the artist, carried out his strange ritual.

In spite of the commotion that persisted down below, David had turned on all the lights in his studio. In defiance of his accusers, he spread out four different paintings of the Virgin on the floor. He undressed himself and began removing lids from paint cans. He lay down on top of the paintings, extending his arms and legs in all directions trying to touch them all at once. He twisted and rolled on top of them, gradually covering each image of the Virgin with a fresh coat of paint. The hours passed when, exhausted, David sensed a presence. In the brilliance of the lights above him, he made out Her delicate face. As She came into full view, She opened up Her gown to expose Her full breasts dripping with sweet milky nourishment. Once more the Virgin offered Herself to David who, finding new strength, feverishly sank his body into Hers. Underneath the burning bright lights of the studio, the two lovers embraced.

From a car parked across the street, a police officer watched over the group that had camped out for the night in front of the gallery. On the sidewalk, the rubble of broken furniture and glass had been piled up for the garbage trucks. In the stillness of the dawn's grey air, the police officer kept his own vigil, flashing his light onto anyone who got too close to the gallery. Then he saw something move inside. He got out of his car, flashlight in hand and, cautiously, made his way over to the gallery's entrance. He looked up at the lit windows in the studio, and then a sound drew his attention back down to the darkness in front of him. He hesitated for a moment, adjusting his gaze as a few of the bystanders gathered behind him. Then, from out of the depths of the gallery a creature emerged, neither human nor beast, struggling to carry four large canvases. They were more of the same abstract paintings, doubtlessly painted over the Virgin of Guadalupe.

"It's him!" one of the onlookers whispered.

With his face caked in blood and his body coated in various colors, David turned to face the invasive light head-on, raising his hand to shield his eyes. Then he crouched down to peer out at the sky's first light. He walked unceremoniously to the broken front window, where he arranged the four paintings in front of everyone who stood with their mouths agape at the sight of the comic and terrible prodigy. With a grotesque smile deformed by a new tumor that had broken out behind his upper lip, David confronted the onlookers who glared at him maliciously. He went to the office, only to return moments later with a fistful of price tags to pin on the paintings: five thousand dollars each. They remained speechless, as David, apparently pleased with his efforts, picked up a broom and began to sweep the gallery floor.

The scene was interrupted only when Craig and Melissa arrived. They promptly escorted David back to his studio and, then they, too, began the task of restoring order to the damaged gallery. Soon, David's apprentices arrived in a van filled with paintings and easels.

"We are proud to hang our paintings in this gallery," Rita declared.

The three students joined in the clean-up effort while, outside, the police officer called for backup as a new crowd began to gather. From across the street people shouted insults up at the studio where they watched for any sign of movement.

"Lucifer!"

"Sinner!"

"Devil worshipper!"

But David, along with his friends, ignored the demonstrators, even the ones who came to lend support.

"We love you, David!"

"God loves you, David. Come pray with us for your salvation."

Then, a familiar voice was heard, "Where's Pri-Prickles? Where's m-my man, Prickles?"

Denny bellowed as he forced his way through to the gallery entrance. When he spied the four new paintings in the front window, he hurried over to inspect them. For the next five minutes he looked them over carefully.

"I want these t-two here for my Pri-Prickles collection."

Denny made a couple of calls and, within half an hour, a team of carpenters had begun reconstructing shelves and window casings. By three in the afternoon a new and improved front window was installed, with bulletproof glass. And, by night's end, some thirty-six hours after the assault on David and his artwork, the gallery was operational, hosting a number of visitors from civil liberties organizations. They had come to show their support of David's freedom of expression.

In contrast, just outside the gallery, his opponents were gaining in numbers. They condemned David and his paintings for his insensitivity to the Latino community's Catholic beliefs. They accused David of blasphemy, claiming that he was ridiculing the traditions and values that the Latino community held so dearly. This point was not lost on David's mother, who had hastened to join her son after she received word of the attack.

"What were you thinking, David? You should be ashamed of what you're doing to our Blessed Virgin."

David could only respond with a gentle smile.

Gloria took him into her arms and whispered, "It doesn't matter, son. I love you no matter what. Do whatever it takes for you to be happy."

Then she drew his attention to the bundles she had carried in. "Look here, my naughty child. I brought you a bunch of my best quilts. You know, you should really start quilting again."

Still recovering from his battered and bruised body, David slept in the next day. When he hobbled down the stairs just before noon, he was reassured to find the gallery fully restored and open for business. Melissa had come to work early and was fielding one phone call after the next. There were so many that Melissa got hold of the apprentices so that they could come help with the phones. Some were calling to harass David and criticize the gallery. Others just wanted to know when it was open and how to get there. Most defended David, declaring their belief in artistic freedom. One of the phone calls was from Denny, who said that he was missing one of the paintings he had just purchased. Either it was still in the gallery or somebody had stolen it when they were loading the truck.

"If it's lost or s-stolen, don' worry, we-we'll . . . uh, Prickles will replace it."

David refused to speak with anyone who phoned. He received invitations for interviews from radio and television stations, and the journalists were lining up at the gallery door. Everyone wanted to see the monster artist, but he just wanted to be left alone. When the opportunity arose, Melissa slipped him out of the gallery and helped him to his car so he could drive off to the distant hills. Surrounded by the peace and quiet of nature, he spent the day there, meditating with his Holy Beloved.

🔭 🔭 🔭

In the back alley of a Latino neighborhood in East Palo Alto, a boy was getting off his bicycle to get a closer look at what appeared to be an old beggar lying against a garbage bin, just in front of a garage that had been converted into an apartment. Frightened by the twisted grimace on his lifeless face and the bright colors on his hands and clothes, the boy ran off to the nearest house. Before long a police car and an ambulance arrived. They looked up and down the alley, but found nothing out of the ordinary. When the medical examiners checked out the body, they declared the man dead at the scene.

"So what happened to this ol' fella?" asked a policeman.

One of the medical examiners jotting down notes replied, "It's hard to say. Look at his face. It's all twisted and stretched. And all this paint. It's still sticky. Very, very strange. Don't you think?"

The scene drew a crowd, neighbors who thought they'd seen the man before could only speculate about the brightly colored paints. When one of the local boys poked around in the garbage bin, something caught his eye. He jumped in and came up with a painting:

"Hey! Look at this! I found where the paint came from!"

One of the policemen took hold of the painting, but, as he turned to show it to the rest of the investigation team, he tripped over one of the medical examiners who was still crouching down to inspect the body. The officer, with the painting stretched out in front of him, landed on top of the deceased, much to the delight of all the kids. There were still a few chuckles as the young officer struggled back to his feet, with a large rainbow-colored smear across his uniform. As he stood there embarrassed and stupefied as to how to clean himself off, a woman shrieked, "Look! Under the painting . . . the body is moving!"

To everyone's amazement, the dead man stretched his legs, lifted the painting off his chest and placed it gently to the side. Lying next to him you could make out the image of the Virgin of Guadalupe underneath a thin smear of bright colors. Upon seeing this, the faithful instinctively crossed themselves. And some began to kneel and pray.

One of the older men exclaimed, "A miracle! It's a miracle! The Virgin brought the dead guy back to life!"

The medical examiner looked at his staff, eyebrows raised. "He was dead. Really, he was."

Bewildered by what had transpired before them, the police and medical personnel just looked at each other and then at the old man who was now sitting up scratching his head. When they insisted that he relax and remain on the ground, the old man became irritated.

"The hell I will! I'm going home! And give me my painting back, you fuckin' assholes!"

The word spread instantly through the Latino community. The crowd had gotten hold of the painting and, by the end of the day, they had erected an altar. The alley began to fill with flowers brought by a steady stream of followers. The authorities had closed off the alley and finally convinced the old man to come away to a hospital. When Denny heard the news, he came to satisfy his suspicion. Sure enough, he recognized the painting surrounded by candles and flowers as the one he had bought a day earlier. He was more than happy to leave it where it was, idolized by a host of believers. As Denny retreated from the scene, he came across more and more people looking for "Virgin Alley." By now, people had returned from work and, hearing the news of the miracle, they were heading out with the whole family to see the Virgin. Then the camera crews arrived.

Whispering under his breath, "Fuckin' Prickles! Look what you've done," Denny smiled as he made his way through the approaching crowd.

On his way back from the foothills, David got stuck in a traffic jam, and it didn't take him long to figure out why. The events surrounding "Virgin Alley" were being broadcast on the radio news. Afraid that someone would recognize him in his car, he ducked down as best he could, and, when he finally made it back to the gallery, he parked a few blocks away and snuck in through the back door. From the gallery front window, Melissa, Craig, the apprentices and Denny were watching a procession as it made its way either to or from "Virgin Alley." David crept up to his studio unnoticed, and then he phoned down.

"It's me, Melissa. I'm here. I'm fine. I'm with my loved one. I'm going to work. You guys go home."

For days, the image of the Virgin and the story of how She had resurrected a dead beggar in an alley made it onto the television news. Reporters described the scene and the painting, but every description was different. It was as if the Virgin Herself were changing Her posture or facial expression. Everyone who went to the altar saw something different. The image of the Virgin, shrouded by a thin coat of bright colors, revealed Herself in different ways to different people. She communicated directly and personally to each of Her followers. Some felt an immediate need to share the message that they had received from the Virgin. Some saw the Virgin with arms outstretched as if to embrace them. Others avowed that the Virgin had smiled at them, instantly filling them with feelings of peace and well-being. These people came away from the altar radiating joy.

Curiously, some ended up running away, visibly disturbed by what they had seen. Some broke down, screaming that they were sinners, condemned. While some fell to their knees to pray, others hurried off terrified by the punishment that they foresaw in the painting. One man declared that what he witnessed was so horrible that it defied description. He insisted that the Virgin had shown him this as a sign of the coming Apocalypse.

Reporters followed anyone who came away noticeably affected by their encounter with the Virgin. But none of these people were willing to describe their experience in detail. They finally convinced one woman, who had fainted from what she saw in the painting, by promising a sum of money in exchange for her testimonial. At first she refused to speak on camera, but after they offered her more money, she consented to being filmed in the presence of a priest.

"Everyone knows that I'm a respectable woman, devoted to the Church and to my family," she said. "All the good priests and sisters from the parish know me. I don't know why the Virgin of Guadalupe chose me to see such filthy perverted acts. But now, through me, my mouth, my lips, my tongue, She has a message for the world:

I like to make love just like any other woman. I like to feel the flesh of my lovers against my skin, and inside me. I want to touch their thighs and hold their throbbing organs overflowing with love. It is my loving duty to open my mouth to their passionate kisses and their sacred human juices. We come together in the name of God. His sacred spirit comes to life in the body of needy men who yearn to love me and Him. I am the one to guide them to His love. I am the holy Virgin of Guadalupe, whose naked body a humble artist covered one night under a rainbow of colors."

The woman's words ended abruptly as if she had awoken from a trance. Then David, naked and covered in paint, turned off the television.

The notoriety of "Prickles, the monster artist" forced David into even more of a hermit's life, a prisoner of his own success, locked away in his private studio, where he produced abstract paintings that veiled the Virgin of Guadalupe's warm body. As if to further incite his detractors, he would produce the occasional work with just a glimpse of a body part showing through. He could not leave the gallery, because they were all waiting for him, to see him and to touch him. Getting in and out of the gallery even became difficult for Melissa. Ultimately she was forced to hire private bodyguards to protect David and his associates. With so much attention paid to him, David's reputation as an artist, and the value of his art work, soared. Joining in Melissa's efforts to foster David's talent, Craig and Denny became more and more involved in the gallery's activities. Denny purchased land adjoining the Stanford campus, where he oversaw the construction of a conservatory that served as an extension of the gallery. David would go there to rest and to host visits from his mother or aspiring artists seeking admittance to his workshop, which, by then, had been turned over to the original three apprentices: Rita, Eduardo and Ronaldo.

🐜 🐜 🐜

As time went by, the debates continued over the rights and responsibilities of artists. At the center of the debate was David, who chose to remain silent through it all, speaking only through his paintings and, on his mother's advice, his renewed enthusiasm for quilting. At Stanford and other nearby institutions, the case of the deformed artist who defiled the Virgin of Guadalupe, the most sacred image in the pantheon of Mexican

Catholicism, would provoke discussion and divide opinions for many years to come.

David was accused of being an atheist and a sell-out to the Anglos who controlled the art world from New York. Some critics decided that Prickles, just like any other Chicano or Chicana artist, had compromised his values to gain access to national and international markets. Those who defended him argued that artists should be free to express themselves however they wished, and that was precisely what Prickles had done. Even MEChA, Stanford's Chicano student activist organization, was divided. Discussions were so heated that, one night, the opposing sides came to blows. The fight happened during a party at the Casa Zapata, a student dorm that housed many Chicano activists. An argument in front of the residence quickly turned into a brawl. They were beating the hell out of each other to a pulp until a nauseating juicy thud, like when you split open a watermelon, brought the fighting to a halt. A moment later the panic broke out from the sight of a young student lying in a pool of blood with a metal crucifix embedded in his skull. Some crazy bastard had decided to take the debate to the next level. The news of the fallen student produced such an outrage that, not long afterward, a march was organized that began at the murder scene and ended outside the gallery's doors. Once again the police were called in to protect the gallery and other local businesses from rioters.

The debate raged throughout the Latino community, and, eventually, spilled over into the Anglo world. For the first time, Latinos were vociferous. That is, every Latino was reacting to David's paintings: either for or against. In the meantime, David's condition worsened. His tumors grew bigger and more painful than ever before. But his relationship with the Virgin continued nonetheless. And he continued to make a fortune from his paintings, though he sometimes complained that, as a consequence, he could never go out in public.

He was interviewed by Barbara Walters, who asked, "Why do you paint abstract designs over the Virgin of Guadalupe? Rumors are that in some of your paintings the Virgin is engaged in some pretty controversial acts. Why do you do this?"

David, with his body hunched over, and his face cruelly deformed, spoke in a slow, deliberate voice: "I paint because my Loved One, the Virgin of Guadalupe, commands it. She is my Goddess. She is my salvation. I must obey Her commands. Nobody can or will take Her gift away from me. She loves me and I love Her. I have dedicated my life and my art to the Virgin of Guadalupe, and no one can deny this sacred relationship."

🐜 🐜 🐜

Whenever I stayed over at my mother's house, I slept in my usual spot: in the living room underneath a painting of the Virgin of Guadalupe. It had always been there, but it wasn't until later in life that I had taken any notice of it. When I drew nearer to admire the exquisite detail of the Sacred Mother's sublime expression, I saw it: at Her feet there was a little angel with thorns protruding from his face and body, with a name inscribed on his forehead: "Prickles."

Little Nation

The only thing we can do is build our own little nation.
We know that we have complete control in our community.
It's like we're making our stand and we're able to express
ourselves this way. We're all brothers and nobody fucks
with us. . . . We take pride in our own little nation and
if any intruders enter, we get panicked because we feel
our community is being threatened. The only
way is with violence.
—Cholo from Ontario

Criminality in this country is a class issue. Many of those
warehoused in overcrowded prisons can be properly called
"criminals of want," those who've been deprived of the
basic necessities of life and therefore forced into so-called
criminal acts to survive. Many of them just don't have
the means to buy their "justice."
—Luis J. Rodríguez

The town of Nuestra Señora la Reina de Los Ángeles was
founded by mestizos, mulatos, Indians and a French albino
on the banks of the Porciúncula River in the year 1781. After
months of struggling to survive in the newly formed town, only
a few of the original founders remained. From them was born
an intense desire to stay and to see the little town grow. They

were not prepared to abandon the land granted to them by the Mexican government as recompense for the long and perilous journey they had risked. These pioneers would stay. Nothing and no one could force them to leave. There in the town they worked, they had children and raised families. There they lived, died and were buried. Into each of the dearly departed souls that they buried in the earth, roots took hold, roots that nourished the fields, the animals and the next generation. The love and the labor that went into the land gave them the right to declare that it belonged to them, and they were prepared to die defending it. They never abandoned nor fled from the town of Nuestra Señora la Reina de Los Ángeles.

Prior to the year 1842, anyone who died there was buried in the San Gabriel Mission Cemetery. The first graveyard was located at the north end of the plaza church. It served the community's needs for generations, but, by the 1840s, a group of residents had presented a petition at the L.A. town hall meeting, declaring that the graveyard was no longer adequate for the growing population. It posed a danger to the community's health. You could no longer dig a grave there for your departed loved ones without offending your neighbors. More specifically, the graveyard was so full of bodies that you could not break earth with a spade or a pickax without striking the skull, leg or arm of a cadaver that was "resting in peace." A few times when they moved one interred body to make room for another, the rank odor of the former leached through the disturbed earth and, especially on hot days, wafted through the whole town.

The situation never improved. It reached a point where those in mourning began laying the dead to rest on their own lands, establishing family burial grounds. After the wake, every family would put on a grand celebration in their own homes, a commemoration to honor the dead with food, drink and testimonials. When they awoke the next day, they would cure their hangovers with more of the same poison. With drink they eased the pain of a lost loved one and found courage to take the deceased to the gravesite that had been prepared earlier by neighbors and relatives. Some chose sites out in the fields, far away from town. Others preferred a site in the foothills, or beneath a cluster of trees, or next to a stream. There were even graveyards designated for those who died without family. These were often found at the side of an isolated road, or by a busy highway, so that the soul of the deceased could continue on its way in search of the lost family. Sometimes an enormous rock, a precipice or the bend in a river marked the site of a burial ground.

At the foot of a hill on the outskirts of Montebello there stood an enormous oak tree that you could spot from miles away. When children went by the tree in the daytime they would recount the story of the Indian who refused to abandon the surrounding lands. The Indian, after his wife and five children were murdered for resisting the authorities, after they burned down his house, killed his livestock and cut down his corn fields, retreated to the tree where, sheltered by its giant branches, he sat down to contemplate all that he had loved so dearly and worked so hard to create. The Indian loved the land, and he refused to abandon the souls of his wife and children. The white men and the Mexicans had burned the bodies, leaving their bones to smolder with the ashes from the ranch. Braced against the tree, he would watch over his family in the afterlife until he joined them, until he became a spirit. He would haunt his lands until someone gave them a proper Catholic burial. With his back pressed firmly against the trunk, he sat motionless. When the townsfolk passed by they would see him there staring into the distance. The Indian just sat there with his eyes fixed on the ranch and on the ashes of his loved ones that swirled up in the wind. The neighbors would often pass by the tree, but no one ever offered to help him or give him water.

They were unable to see through their own veils of ignorance, fear and bitterness.

Over time the Indian sank deeper and deeper into the base of the tree, until tree and Indian were one. The two watched over the ruins and the desiccated bones. Together as one, they felt the breeze that carried the dust of the deceased. The Indian had disappeared entirely, as if swallowed whole by the tree, but his image appeared in the trunk, high up in the branches, in the leaves or in the roots and the earth itself.

People would only go by in daytime, careful not to get too close to the tree. Children especially would keep their distance. Any gust of wind or sudden noise would send them off running and screaming, "The Indian! The Indian!"

They said that, at night, the Indian would come out from the tree, or from the earth, to work at his ranch. A few foreigners reported that they had stopped at a settlement inhabited by an Indian family. They said that when they arrived at night, hungry and exhausted from a long day's journey, the family offered them food and a place to rest their weary bones. But in the morning, the foreigners woke up to find themselves not in the comfortable beds where they had fallen asleep but on a death bed of smoldering ashes that burned through their clothes, singeing their skin. Some of these foreigners lost their sanity. The others ran off as quickly as possible, terrified by the tree that called to them, pleading with them to come back for a farewell embrace. And so it was that no one ever went near the tree at night, and, even by day, people kept a safe distance.

🐜 🐜 🐜

Bishop Mora faced the L.A. City Council and explained that, given the city's continued urban sprawl and the need for improved sanitation, his church had decided on some fifty acres

of land to the east of Los Angeles, in Boyle Heights, to be sanc-
tified for a Catholic cemetery. Bishop Mora, along with his
priests and numerous parishioners, presented their plan to the
council, and it was approved, receiving unanimous support
from the L.A. Board of Health. But due to pressure from the
powerful American Protection Association, Bishop Mora was
forced to make an executive decision, whereby he changed the
location from Boyle Heights to a property further out from the
city. The American Protection Association had protested
because it did not want the remains from an old cemetery trans-
ferred to the luxurious Boyle Heights neighborhood. Its
representative also pointed out that a cemetery where Mexican
Catholics or non-white Catholics were buried would lower the
property values and tarnish Boyle Heights' reputation as an
upper-class community. For this reason, and also because half
of the members of the association were women whose husbands
donated generously to Bishop Mora's order, the bishop decided
on an alternate location for the cemetery. And so it happened
that Calvary Cemetery was established beyond the city limits,
on Whittier Street in East L.A. And it was here that Micaela
Clemencia, a school teacher interested in local history, strolled
quietly in contemplation of some of the older gravestones
while, a little farther off, a priest mourned with the family of a
seven-year-old girl who had been killed in the crossfire of gang
warfare.

As many as two thousand people from the local community paid their respects as they passed her coffin. During the wake
two days earlier, the residents of East L.A. had brought flowers,
food and donations to the family. People were fed up with the
killings in their streets, with the innocent victims who fell daily
in a sudden flurry of bullets. People were disheartened, out-
raged and furious with the police, who seemed to take no
interest in the murder of a child, a teenager, a Mexican. The

community felt that it had no police protection at all, that no efforts were being made to apprehend the killers, to bring them to justice and to make them pay for their crimes with life imprisonment or a death sentence.

It was Micaela's opinion that the police and the sheriffs of L.A. County were there just to make sure that the Latinos did not leave the area and to ensure the free circulation of drugs and alcohol, thereby maintaining a high rate of criminal activity. In this way they justified their positions, their jobs as investigators, patrolmen and prison guards for the County of L.A. It was no secret that the union representing police and prison guards had contracted the most powerful and influential agencies to protect their interests within national and state governments. The police and other anti-criminal organizations justified their existence in correlation to the growing crime rates. And this situation was not unique to Latino communities. The same theory was also applied to Asian and African-American neighborhoods.

It was Sunday morning, and Micaela was placing flowers at the foot of a tombstone. The scent of red roses mixed with the smell of warm asphalt that rose from the narrow cemetery roads, heated by the springtime sun. A few of her neighbors recognized her and waved with a customary "good morning." In effect, they all knew who she was because of her recent activity, her efforts to organize the community against the proposal to reclaim one hundred and fifty acres located in the heart of East L.A., to build two new stadiums: one for an NFL franchise, another for a soccer league.

"The Los Angeles Latino population loves soccer. They'll be willing to sell their land," the mayor had declared publicly, accompanied by two Latino advisors from the county.

This wouldn't be the first time that the county or the city repossessed properties or houses from Mexicans, declaring them to be uninhabitable and using the right of "eminent domain" to construct a stadium. The case of Chávez Ravine was still fresh in the memory of Mexicans.

ॐ ॐ ॐ

Micaela Clemencia was a teacher at the Santa Teresa de Jesús Primary School in East L.A. As a young girl she had received her early schooling from Benedictine nuns at a convent in Montebello, California. She studied philosophy, theology, literature, history, languages, math and science. Later in life, following the advice of her teacher, Sister Mary Benita Gibbons, she continued her studies at Loyola Marymount in Los Angeles, not far from where she was born. There, Micaela would study with Sister Catarina Triger, a practitioner of liberation theology developed from a grass-roots movement. This ideology was founded on three principles: "observation," which demands a recognition of the reality of the world around us and of souls in crisis; "analysis," which requires delving into the crisis to find out its causes, while proposing a plan to resolve it; and "action," which means doing whatever it takes to help, just as Jesus Christ would take action to achieve beneficial changes for human salvation. Sister Catarina was a great admirer of the writer and French educator Louise Michel (1830-1905).

Micaela had very few memories of her parents. What she did remember was that her father drove a big truck for a living, an eighteen-wheeler that he would run from California to Arizona, New Mexico, Colorado, Nevada, Oklahoma, Utah and Oregon, returning through the Imperial Valley to arrive back at Montebello, where they lived on Date Street. She remembered the many times he took her and her mom on the really long trips that would last for weeks, loading and unloading goods throughout the entire American Southwest. She knew that they were big trucks because her father would often park them in front of the house before reporting to the company's central office on Vail Street. He worked for Pacific Intermountain Express. The image of her father jumping down from a huge red truck and of herself wiggling away from her mother to go running into her father's outstretched arms would be forever etched in her memory. Gonzalo and Natividad Clemencia, Micaela's parents, were buried in the Calvary Cemetery.

Micaela remembered that spring afternoon when Sister Mary Benita Gibbons came to get her out of class. Micaela was in grade two at the time.

"I'm sorry," Sister Mary said, "but I have some bad news to tell you."

She took Micaela by the hand and led her to her office. Sister Mary brought her a drink and then sat down beside her to explain that her parents wouldn't be able to come for her, ever again. "How do you explain to a child that her parents have died in a car accident?" thought Sister Mary. But as she was thinking of a strategy, two police officers and a woman in a blue suit entered the office. The woman appeared exaggeratedly professional. The three strangers sat down and listened as Sister Mary explained that because there had been an accident, the policemen and the lady had come for her. In the end, however, Sister Mary convinced the court to allow her to care for Micaela at the convent.

And so it was that Micaela's fate was to be orphaned at seven years of age and to be raised by nuns at St. Benedict's Convent in Montebello, California. Over time, everyone became aware of the tragedy that had taken the lives of the girl's parents. The parishioners all agreed, however, that the girl was fortunate to find a home with the nuns. Although there were several couples interested in adopting her, families both rich and poor that wanted to take her in, Sister Mary categorically refused to allow it. Thus, Micaela grew up under her tutelage. The parishioners decided that, because she was an exceptional student, her educational privileges should continue. Accordingly, they established an education fund in her name. Wealthy families would often invite her to spend the weekend with them, where she would get to swim in their pool and eat filet mignon from the grill. Poor families from Simons, southeast of the city, or the Jardín neighborhood to the south, also got their chance to host weekend visits from Micaela, when she would be invited to partake in large weddings, *quinceañeras* and neighborhood barbecues. Both rich and poor families were happy to contribute to Micaela's education.

ꗇ ꗇ ꗇ

By the time she celebrated her fifteenth birthday, Micaela was already a young lady. She grew tall and thin, with thick straight hair. Her forehead was high and broad. Her eyes were brown and almond shaped, with droopy eyelids. She had a pointy nose with wide nostrils, an extended groove over her upper lip and thin lips that rarely smiled. But when she did laugh, the sun radiated from her, illuminating her whole face.

In the middle of the playground at St. Benedict's School, Sister Mary sat down with Micaela to reveal her future plans and to hand over a few gifts that her parents had left her. It was on an afternoon just like this one eight years earlier when Sister Mary had told Micaela about what had happened to her parents.

"Your parents loved you very much. They were smart people who planned for your future. What I will say and give you today is their legacy to you," Sister Mary said, taking Micaela's hands into hers.

"Your father, a truck driver, through the advice of the owner of the trucking company that employed him, invested in the stock market before you were born. He purchased major stocks like Mobil, Microsoft and Intel. All of these stocks have risen substantially in value. Today they are in your name and in mine as your legal guardian. At first the Church denied me the right to be your legal guardian, but I threatened to leave the order, and they eventually backed down. The stocks will revert completely to you on your twenty-first birthday. Until then I serve as executrice of the estate. Also, there is the matter of the church fund established for you by the many people who love you. That money has also grown to a sizeable amount. You probably don't understand what all this means, but you must know that your parents loved you and provided for you. You are very lucky to have had parents with such foresight. Not many working-class people think like your parents did. I wish more Mexicans would think like them. I learned from a parishioner that your mother earned money as a domestic worker, cleaning houses. Nothing to be ashamed of, Micaela. You should be proud of people who work. And your parents were hard workers, builders always creating something good for you," Sister Mary concluded as she ran her fingers through the girl's long hair.

"I am proud of my parents, Sister Mary," was Micaela's reply.

"I know you are, dear. That's why I am going to give you this," Sister Mary said as she opened an envelope and took out some photos. "I have saved these for you, for the right time, which God has told me is now. I know that you do not have photos of your parents. I'm sorry that these photos were taken after your parents' deaths, at the wake and the funeral," she said, handing the photos to Micaela.

"I don't remember my parents' faces."

"These photos were used as evidence against the drunk driver who ran the red light going sixty miles per hour."

"I don't have many memories of them. Thank you, with these I can remember their faces and imagine their bodies moving. But I don't remember the wake or the funeral."

"Hundreds and hundreds of people came. You stood by me. You never cried. Have you ever cried for your parents, Micaela?"

"I don't remember crying for anything. Is that bad, Sister?"

"Only if you hold back tears, my dear. It isn't healthy to hold back tears. You will only drown in your silent sorrow. Please, Micaela, don't let that happen to you." Sister Mary handed her more photos, some that the police had taken to identify and describe her parents' broken bodies. When she realized what she was about to show Micaela, she pulled them back and clutched them against her chest.

"I'm sorry, Micaela. But I felt that I should give you these photos. I'm sorry. Please forgive me!" Sister Mary wept.

Micaela gave her a hug and assured her that by seeing the images she would be able to move forward, that her parents were still with her, now more than ever.

"Thank you, Micaela. You are kind and appreciative. God has blessed you with many gifts. There is one in particular that I must tell you about now, and I hope that you will accept it."

"Your gifts are wonderful, Sister. Coming from you they must be God's will."

"I'm glad you feel that way, my dear. This gift I have never mentioned to you before. It represents the only wish and request I have of you. You are fifteen years of age and soon you must think about going away to study at a university. My wish is that you go study for several years with the Benedictine nuns at Kylemore Abbey before you enter an American university."

"Sister, that's where you studied to become a teacher! I want to go, yes, I will go!" Micaela replied enthusiastically, having heard so many of Sister Mary's stories about her days in Ireland.

"Upon your return, Micaela, all that I have described will be yours, and you will be free to attend whichever university you choose. All this will help you do God's good work."

⁂

A week after the funeral for the young girl who had been killed at the hands of gangsters, Micaela was arriving home, tired and faint from hunger. That morning she had been in such a hurry that she had skipped breakfast, and then the parent-teacher interviews ran late, well beyond the lunch hour. She had consumed nothing more than half a doughnut with two cups of coffee. When she opened the fridge she found nothing that appealed to her. She went back out again and headed to Costa's store, just a block away.

Micaela walked briskly because she wanted to pass unnoticed by Doña Felícitas and Doña Paca. She knew that if they spotted her, they would hold her up to talk about their rheumatism, their husbands and how things were in the neighborhood way back when. Micaela knew the last words of any conversation with these respected elderly ladies. She had these final words on her mind as she walked in front of their house.

"You know what kids need these days?"

"I sure do, Paca, a good spanking on their bottoms."

Micaela raced by until she was beyond their reach. Nothing happened in the neighborhood without their knowing. They knew who was pregnant, who was kicked out of the house, who was feuding, who was rich, who was poor, who could read, who had relatives living with them illegally. They knew these things not so much because they were gossipy, but, rather, because everyone went to them to talk about their problems, as if at the confessional.

The two ladies were widows who, after their husbands died, went back to school to take accounting classes and learn how to prepare federal and state taxes. They made a living from it. They worked like the scribes of old, writing letters and filling out official documents for locals who could neither read nor write.

They had all the equipment they needed to operate their business from home: computers, printers, photocopier and fax machine, and telephones everywhere you looked. They were connected to the Internet and had electronic access to local universities. It was an impressive setup that grew over the years with the accumulating files. They even built an addition that connected their two homes and served as a library.

Micaela had been in their home many times. They had invited her over for tea—they didn't drink coffee. After two or three hours of discussing the new tax laws that could affect local residents, or why rosebushes grew tall with vibrant colors on some properties and not others, Micaela would take her leave, exhausted and somewhat dizzy from the ladies' endless verbal onslaught.

Going by their house Micaela was careful not to be captured by these two women she considered to be extremely intelligent, but also somewhat eccentric.

With the danger behind her, she began to slow her pace when, all of a sudden, she saw them up ahead running toward her.

"Is everything okay, ladies?"

"Micaela, there's been a shooting! At the Costa store," Felícitas huffed.

"I'm going for the cameras. Felícitas, you get the tape recorders," Paca commanded.

The two ladies left Micaela standing alone facing the oncoming lights: yellow, red, white and blue. In the time that it

took her to walk cautiously the rest of the way to Costa's, ten
more police cars had arrived, black and white ones from the
L.A. County Sheriff's Department. They were parked in the
middle of the road, with officers leaning up against the doors
making casual conversation. Some of them, having realized that
too many officers had shown up, got back into their cars and
sped away.

"Once again they've invaded our neighborhood," Micaela
thought as she lost count of all the police cars. Here they were
again rushing into the neighborhood with an exaggerated convoy of squad cars and paddy wagons. As usual, they arrived
late. When there's a murder around here, they either ignore it or
respond when the body is already stiff and cold. The officers
hover around the victim pretending to be concerned, but, really, what do they care about another death in this neighborhood?
Their procedures are inconsistent and do little to deter crime in
the area. This way they guarantee themselves a job. Their interest in the community picks up when reporters show up to do
interviews and to film or photograph the crime scene. The
police and the press team up to sort out the details of the scan-
dalous criminal element that, according to them, pervades the
Latino neighborhoods of Los Angeles. All they do is create a
growing distrust between the community and the police force,
and they've also aggravated tensions between Latino communities and between the various crime agencies themselves. As a
result, people from the barrio have grown increasingly wary of
all public institutions.

Micaela noticed that Doña Paca was filming everything
with her video camera while Doña Felícitas shadowed the
investigators with a microphone, recording their every word.
The police didn't take any notice of the two old ladies, allowing them to move about the crime scene unimpeded. The many
sheriffs who were Latino made an obvious effort to steer clear

of the two ladies. Little by little, Micaela drew closer to the open doors at the back of a van. Inside she saw the body of a girl of about fifteen or sixteen years of age. She was lying on her back, naked, with her unshaven legs bent and twisted. Micaela could make out that the girl's face was blue with grossly swollen lips, and there was a dried trickle of blood from her nose.

"The sons of bitches did her and strangled her. Where's the fuckin' lab boys?"

"They're having trouble coming up the road."

"Well, move those units out of the way, dammit!"

Doña Paca watched the scene unfold through the camera eye, and Felícitas heard it all through her tape recorder's ear phones. Micaela observed the horribly motionless girl, the detectives who refused to cover the body for fear of disturbing evidence, the cops who came over to see the murder victim for themselves and now the local residents who had crowded together here and there, murmuring who they thought the victim might be.

Out of nowhere a young woman ran toward the back of the van screaming hysterically. "Cover her, for Christ's sake, put something over her!"

"Fuck! Where'd she come from?"

"Sorry, Lieutenant. I tried to stop her. But she bolted from her car."

"Those bastards will pay!" she cried. "I know who they are, and I'll kill every one of them sons of whores!"

"Get her the hell out of here!"

Three female officers forced her into a squad car and took off with the siren blaring. Perhaps she was a sister, Micaela thought.

As the car drove away, Micaela realized that only one reporter, accompanied by a cameraman, had shown up.

Hovering in the sky there were a couple of press helicopters, each from one of the big TV stations, and a helicopter from the sheriff's department. The next morning there wasn't a single mention of the incident in the papers. Murders in a Latino neighborhood were simply not newsworthy. They were so common that editors paid little to no attention to the death of another gangster, or to another random victim of gang violence. They were never covered by the TV news and only rarely in the newspapers, in which case they were usually relegated to the back pages. The constant killings were of no interest to anyone outside the barrio.

The news spread through the community by word of mouth that the murder was an act of revenge between rival gangs. They killed the girl because her boyfriend's gang had crossed over into their territory to sell drugs. Drugs remain a constant problem because police allow them to circulate throughout the barrio. The authorities talk out of both sides of their mouths, declaring that they are constantly fighting against drug trafficking, but they also say that the law doesn't allow them to do anything until they catch traffickers in the act. They know who is responsible for poisoning our youth, but they won't apprehend them. They just keep them under observation.

Micaela wanted to know more. What she discovered was that this was another case of mistaken identity. The girl who was murdered had been confused with the friend she was visiting that afternoon. This friend had brothers who were members of a gang from Geraghty. The girl that Micaela had seen running to the back of the van crying, the one they took away, was the one they were after.

The victim did not belong to any gang. She was a high school student, and she and the other girl had been hanging out together since they were little kids. The neighbors said that they had seen the two of them talking that day, that the victim was just hanging out at her friend's house, but this was enough to make her a target. About five homeboys abducted her, took her to the Superior Grocery Store parking lot, where they drugged her and raped her. When they were done, they strangled her and ditched the body in a van in front of Costa's. These kinds of gangsters represent only a small percentage of the youth growing up in our community. But these monsters are the only ones who ever receive any publicity. In the news they would never think to mention that the majority of Latino teenagers respect the law, that the majority is studying or working hard to improve their lives and the lives of their families. Absolutely no attention is paid to these good kids.

After chatting with some of the locals, Micaela realized that they knew who the murderers were. Two of them were among the spectators during the police investigation. People knew their names, but they would never come forward for fear of retaliation. Even the victim's parents chose not to give their names. The father, a religious man, spoke not of vengeance but instead of forgiving the young criminals.

"I know who the boys are who killed my daughter. God will punish them, and He will forgive them. It's now in the hands of our Father," the man said, speaking with Micaela.

"What are their names?" Micaela asked.

"No. Young lady, I'm not looking for revenge," was his reply. Then he went back into his house and closed the door behind him. Inside you could hear his wife crying.

For a moment, standing there in silent frustration, she thought that they didn't care that these murderers roamed free, alive and well while their daughter lay dead, silenced forever. They were afraid that if they did identify the murderers to the police, the gangsters would come after them. And it didn't matter if you were young or old, an adult or a child, a man or woman. If you sang, you would pay the price.

Obsessed now with the death of the girl and with the fear that pervaded the community, Micaela went to see Paca and Felícitas. Distraught, she walked in and found herself looking around as if it were her first time in the house. The hardwood floors were covered here and there with throw rugs placed in no particular order. The sofas and leather chairs were half-covered by knitted blankets and decorative cushions. There were old lamps with faded lampshades as well as the latest in track lighting, old-fashioned furniture combined with a more modern style. Every object in the house had a practical purpose. The walls in Doña Paca's house were covered with photographs of people from around the neighborhood. Paca had captured on film the physical development and demographic growth of the entire community. There were photos of houses and of the families that lived in them. She took photos of newborns and the elderly. She took her camera to weddings, baptisms, *quinceañeras*, wakes and funerals. Paca had photos of great triumphs and crushing defeats, of happy moments and times of sadness. The walls were covered with history, and the faces of the barrio watched you as you visited her home.

"Come on in, Micaela! We're in the library," Felícitas called out.

Paca had also begun displaying her photos on Felícitas's walls. There was always an occasion for a photo, and Paca always gave a free copy to her subjects. There was no doubt about Paca's passion for capturing and recording local history. Felícitas was equally obsessed, but her passion was computers. She had them in every room, along with photocopiers, printers, scanners and fax machines. She also kept an assortment of telephones and shortwave radios.

As she climbed the stairs to the library, Micaela saw photos of Paca, Felícitas and their husbands. In the photos, Paca's husband was always carrying a camera. Jesús Gaylen Saragoza was one of the first Mexican filmmakers to work in Hollywood. He had been trained in the Churubusco Studios in Mexico City before pursuing his career in the United States. There were many photos of Felícitas' husband in front of computers or radio equipment. Her husband, Ramón Arom, was a Mexican engineer. He had studied at the University of Southern California and was one of the first to work in computer manufacturing. He worked mainly with communication systems, radio in particular. In many of the photos the two couples were posing in front of impressive landscapes and buildings in far-off lands. It looked as if they had traveled to every corner of the world. Both men were handsome and always smiling.

Micaela walked into the library, where she found Paca dismantling a motion detector, while Felícitas read quietly.

"I want to know the names of the boys who raped and killed that girl."

It was then that Micaela suddenly realized how angry she was.

🐜 🐜 🐜

Micaela was on her way back from the district attorney's office, where she brought forward the names and photos of the murderers. The detectives and police officers with whom she spoke said that they had had these guys under surveillance for almost a year. They knew that they were present at the time of the murder, but they couldn't arrest them based on hearsay. What they needed was a statement from an eyewitness or some form of hard evidence. The authorities admitted that the gangsters that Micaela had identified were the killers, but they hastened to add that they were not in any position to apprehend them.

"So what good are you? You know who the killers are, but you allow them to roam free so they can kill again. You try to control our community by using fear. You don't protect us, you just keep us corralled by leaving killers on the streets. That's how you operate. You depend on our fear. You know what these criminals are doing, but you choose to do nothing about it. But when one of your own dies, you waste no time in finding the murderer. If the victim is a poor Mexican girl, or black, Asian or homosexual, then you just make a note of it for your files, another statistic to prove that gangs are running rampant through poor neighborhoods." Micaela snarled in disgust as she left the office.

It was late afternoon and Micaela was still angry, still trying to figure out why the police took no action against such brutal killers. She was climbing the hill toward her house when, over by Costa's store, under the shade of an enormous apricot tree, she saw them. The young homeboys who had just raped and killed a girl were hanging out in their usual spot. There were five of them, along with two smaller children. When the two younger kids caught sight of Micaela coming toward them, they immediately threw their cigarettes behind them.

"Hey, that's a whole joint, you little shit!"

Micaela recognized the two little ones. They were students of hers, a boy and a girl who were frequently absent from school. She had tried calling their parents, but the father was in prison and the two jobs that their mother worked kept her out of the house until midnight. The eighty-year-old grandmother was the only one looking after them. They didn't have a house. Instead they stayed at the dilapidated Saddlehorse Hotel. These kids lived in perpetual poverty, likely traumatized by what went on around them. They suffered emotionally and from physical hunger. They had problems sleeping. When they did show up for class, quite often they would doze off, and whenever Micaela woke them up they would become hostile.

Upon seeing them, Micaela called over. "Lunita, Edgar!" She stamped out the joint that still smoldered at their feet. The homeboys were laughing at them.

"They're fucked up!"

"Crazy lil' bastards!"

The two children put on a brave face in front of the homeboys, but Micaela saw right through them.

"Either I see you in class tomorrow morning or I'm coming to get you," she warned them, aware that they weren't listening to a word she said.

"It looks like these two have already been lost," she thought to herself as she turned to face the homeboys.

"You shouldn't mess with these kids. Just stay away from them. And I know what you did to that girl," she boldly declared to the five young men who now surrounded her.

"Everybody knows, *ésa.*"

"So, what's new?" they laughed.

"Just stay away from my children. You hear me?"

"We'll stay away if we want to stay away. This is our barrio and we make the rules. Ain't that right, Javier?"

"Fuck yeah, Celicio. We rule, and there ain't nobody can do a fuckin' thing about it, little woman!"

"I'm sick of you punks," Micaela said. "And I'm warning you now. I'm going to get you for that murder!"

"You're fucked up, little lady. You better watch it or you're gonna be a dead teacher," Celicio replied in a low voice, gesturing a gun shot from his hand.

Celicio lit a cigarette and motioned to his homies that it was time to go. Not one of them looked back as they sauntered over to Costa's. They went in and came out with six packs of beer. Two of them walked up the hill, while Celicio and two others got into a big Cadillac, where they broke out the booze. Micaela could hear them talking and laughing as they guzzled one beer after another. They were your classic homeboys, wearing baggy pants with tight white tank tops, all except Celicio, who wore a white and blue plaid shirt with long sleeves. This style of clothing was their way of identifying themselves as members of a gang, and it warned others to look away. They finished their beer and threw the empties out near a garbage can. One of them staggered out, then the big Cadillac drove off.

The boy who got out of the car walked right past Micaela, oblivious to her presence. The three or more beers that he had just downed in less than fifteen minutes had given him a good buzz. He stumbled against a fence and stood there for a moment gazing through the chain link. As he held on to the fence with one hand, his free arm swung like a pendulum. Then, with a Herculean effort, he yanked himself up and over, landing on a small patch of grass beside a worn path, a shortcut across the hill. Micaela watched as the boy lumbered up the path and disappeared into silence on the other side.

🐜 🐜 🐜

Upon Micaela's request, Paca and Felícitas located Celicio's car: a big, fully loaded green Cadillac. He parked it under a tarp that hung between an old yellow house and two rickety posts that stood in the long grass of the front yard. This is where he lived with his grandmother.

Around two in the afternoon, Micaela returned from school and immediately set out for Felícitas and Paca's house. A few ignorant tourists stood in front taking pictures. The house had been featured in an article published in the magazine supplement of the *Los Angeles Times*. It identified previously unknown curiosities around Los Angeles that boasted an unusual architecture or history, or eccentric residents. Felícitas and Paca's house met all of these criteria. According to the journalist, "The connected houses are owned by two lovely ingenious seniors. They keep adding to the structures, creating a kind of medieval castle in the middle of East Los Angeles."

Felícitas and Paca were talking about the article when Micaela walked into the kitchen. After a casual greeting, the three women sat down and drank tea in silence. It was time. They went out to the garage to fill the truck with all that they needed, and then they headed out toward Whittier Boulevard. They decided to drive all the way to Montebello, where they stopped for a dinner of stew and meatballs at El Rafael restaurant. They leisurely ate their supper and waited until about nine before asking for the bill. They slowly made their way back to East L.A., climbing the curved hills of their beloved barrio. They pulled over a block away from their destination and looked at one another. It was decided. They drove by the house once to make sure that it was the green Cadillac. By eleven-thirty most people had turned out their lights.

"I've got the matches. Now, Felícitas, you put on the gloves and get the gasoline," Micaela said.

The three women carefully made their way over to Celicio's Cadillac. Paca got the camera ready as Felícitas poured gasoline over the car. She shook the last drops out of the jerry can, then scurried past Micaela, whispering, "Throw the match!"

From across the street Paca photographed the burning car. It only took seconds before it was completely consumed in flames. Felícitas threw her gloves and the jerry can into a cactus thicket and then joined Micaela in the truck. A few minutes later, one of the neighbors ran to Celicio's door.

"Celicio! Your car is on fire!"

The neighbor banged at the door, yelling for Celicio while, in the distance, you could hear the sound of approaching sirens. But the fire had already spread to the canvas connected to the house. By the time Celicio came out carrying his grandmother, half of the building was up in flames. Paca took more photos while Micaela and Felícitas watched from the truck. The neighbors came out to see the little house disappear in the blaze as the roof and walls caved in.

"My house! My house!" Celicio's grandmother cried in despair.

As a few neighbors tried to calm her, the firemen arrived and immediately directed the crowd away from the inferno. Then the Cadillac exploded, shooting the trunk door up into the air, much to the amusement of the onlookers.

When Celicio noticed the smirks and chuckles of his neighbors, he lost it: "Who the fuck burnt my house down! You'll pay for it right fuckin' now! Nobody fucks with me! You hear me, you mother fuckers!"

Two police officers tried to talk to him, but Celicio replied by punching one of them in the face. Then he disappeared under a barrage of night sticks, which continued even after they got the handcuffs on him.

In an hour nothing remained of the house except the charred fridge and stove, and a toilet that stood its ground amid the smoldering ashes. After the firemen doused the last of the embers, they quickly packed up and left with their police escort. Returning to their homes, all the while scolding their excited children, the neighbors could not help but think that God knew how to punish the wicked. Felícitas started up the truck. Micaela waved to some of her students as Paca photographed families retreating to their homes through the garden gates of their little Edens.

By the early morning the smoke permeated the entire neighborhood. And, when Micaela entered her classroom, she felt that her students were looking at her strangely. But she had no regrets. She smiled as she greeted them and got on with the first lesson of the day.

🐜 🐜 🐜

In the twilight of the afternoon, as the clouds changed from red to purple en route to the open Pacific skies, Felícitas and Paca were at Micaela's house talking with the woman who now looked after Celicio's grandmother. They had been in touch with Rebecca Carter, a lawyer from Santa Ana who was a good friend. She was working on negotiating a loan so that the grandmother could have a new house built. The bank did not want to lend her money because her only collateral, in addition to the monthly six hundred dollars of social security, was the lot and the new house to be built.

"But it's in a terrible neighborhood," said the bank loan officer.

It had already gotten dark when Micaela was serving the coffee. Outside they heard the squeal of tires as a car screeched to a halt. Then came the gunshots and the tinkle of broken glass as bullets came through the windows, doors and walls. The women threw themselves to the ground. Seconds later they heard the metallic crunch of a car crash. Without thinking, the women got up and ran out the door. What they saw was a brute of a homeboy pounding Edgar in the face, Micaela's eleven-year-old student.

"You fuckin' idiot, you crashed!" Celicio yelled as he smashed Edgar in the face over and over again.

On impulse Micaela ripped off her blouse and wrapped it around Celicio's neck, choking him and pulling him off of the child. Before he knew it, he was surrounded by the other women and a dozen more who came out of their homes when they realized what was happening. They descended on Celicio, hitting him with brooms, mops, rakes and rocks, whatever they could get their hands on. Celicio got to his feet and tried to grab one of the women, but he was met with ever-increasing blows as the women now numbered close to thirty. He fell to the ground again, trying in vain to shield his head and face from the beating. Lying prostrate, he had lost the fight, and the women stopped just short of beating him unconscious. Helpless, Celicio, the terrorist gangster, murderer and rapist, looked up into the faces of the women who surrounded him, poised to strike again with their domestic weaponry. They knew who he was. They knew about his crimes and that he was trying to kill Micaela or the other women who were in the house that night. Meanwhile the men had come out, but they kept their distance. The fathers, the husbands, the grandfathers and the brothers stood speechless, just looking at one another. No one moved or said a word. All you could hear were Edgar and Celicio moaning in pain.

Finally Edgar's mother arrived and broke into the circle of women. A couple of the neighbors had gone to get her, to force her to come see what had become of her son. When she finally saw him, she yelled, "Call an ambulance! Call the police!"

"No! Don't call anyone!" Micaela shouted, barging in. "We'll look after this one ourselves! What's the police going to do? Nothing!"

Edgar's mother and a few other women helped him into a car and made their way to a hospital.

"Nobody say anything!" another woman yelled out.

"Micaela is right," Felícitas added. "The police know that Celicio is a murderer and they don't do anything about it."

As always, Paca was moving about taking photos of the women who were deliberating over Celicio's fate.

"Strip off his clothes!"

"Undress the rapist!"

Celicio struggled to his feet and managed to strike one of the women as he screamed obscenities and pulled another by the hair. But out of nowhere a sharp handle came down, splitting open his forehead, knocking him back to the ground. They held his limp arms and legs as they undressed him, and one of the women tied his shoelaces around his penis and testicles.

"Let's carry him over to Whittier and dump him in the middle of the street. When they find him there, they'll know what to do with him."

But before they could pick him up, one of the women landed on top of his listless body, looked him in the eyes and spoke: "If we ever see you around here again, we'll kill you. Now, get lost, and give thanks to God that we don't stick a broomstick up your ass and kill you . . . like you did to my daughter!"

Five women lifted Celicio to his trembling feet. His face twisted with the pain of his heavy shoes pulling on his penis and scrotum. He tried to squirm free, but the women held his arms firmly behind his back. They wrapped him in a blanket. They loaded him into the back of a van and left him lying on one of the busiest streets in East L.A. The next day they learned that, naked and struggling to untie the shoes from between his legs, he had staggered onto Whittier Boulevard, where he was hit by a truck and dragged for a block. Celicio died in the county hospital with his grandmother praying the rosary at his side. Even after his death, his grandmother spoke of him as a "good little boy." Yet with nobody to claim the body for burial, his cadaver was incinerated.

🐞 🐞 🐞

In the days that followed, as always seems to be the case after a tragedy, the barrio was quiet. For a few days there was little movement on the once-chaotic dusty streets that Celicio had claimed as his own. In the space where he had lived with his grandmother, all that remained were a few corner posts reduced to black cinders, protruding from a mound of grey

ashes. Throughout the community silence reigned, a grave stillness interrupted only by whispers in private conversations, or a
knowing glance or nod from a neighbor. Every day the men,
women, children and the occasional outsider would walk by the
burnt rubble, pausing for an instant, a moment, an hour, to contemplate the gusts of grey dust and the whiffs of soot and ash.
Satisfied, they would walk away convinced that the community's actions were justified.

Shortly thereafter, the L.A. Sheriff's Department began to
jeopardize this much-needed peace and quiet. The patrol cars
slowed to a stop, their drivers scrutinizing every passerby. They
began stopping people to interrogate them, always ending with
the same question: "Who killed Celicio?"

"Barrio justice" is how Paca replied when she was stopped
on her way home, carrying groceries.

"Who beat up Celicio?" the sheriff asked the woman who
was now caring for his grandmother.

"The fury of female intelligence," she replied under her
breath.

"I want names, lady. How do you expect us to do our job if
you don't tell us who did it?" the sheriff said, raising his voice,
frustrated by the community's enigmatic replies. "Now tell me
who did it, lady!"

"It was a legion of Marías," was all she said as she stepped
back and walked away.

One morning, a group of cops converged on some women
walking their children to school. This time they interrogated the
children.

"Do you kids know who burned down Celicio's house?"

They giggled and replied on cue and in unison, "The good
little children who love their parents!"

Then they ran off chanting their clever reply over and over
again as their mothers smiled knowingly.

The police began to lose patience with the community's wall of silence. Infuriated by their resistance, the police pushed harder and harder to find out who was responsible for Celicio's death, to find the murderer or murderers of the homeboy who terrorized the neighborhood with impunity. People soon became aware of the mounting campaign to squeeze the truth out of the barrio. The police weren't interested in pursuing the investigation of the violent murder of the rape victim. Her life was insignificant compared to Celicio's. They hated him, and they feared him, but Celicio kept the community under control. Along with his gang, Celicio was the father of fear and street violence, of illegitimate children. He provided the drugs, that mystical medicine that seized and corroded the minds of the next generation. Celicio's reign over the barrio substantiated the police presence. He was the accomplice to invasive authority, the guardian of the dominant culture.

The sheriff's department intensified the search, but now, instead of just interrogating people, the police began a photographic file of the barrio. After consulting with county lawyers, they began detaining any teenager they encountered, especially if they appeared to belong to a gang. It was a fiasco from the onset. Whenever young boys saw a cop car, they would stop and wave or slick back their hair and parade around like show girls. Homeboys would adjust their shirts and make sure that their baggy pants hung just over the toe of their shoes, as was the fashion. They wanted to look good for the photo shoot.

"Yo! Over here! Feast your eyes on some bad ass, homeboy booty!" the kids would call over to the squad cars. The police would search them and ask the proverbial question: "Who killed him?"

"The crazy bastards from Geraghty, that's who, *ese,*" the young boys would reply with broad smiles as they horsed around waiting to be photographed.

The police continued with this line of investigation for a couple of months until finally people began to object to the random detention of so many youths, several of whom had been stopped more than once. Some, who had nothing to do with gangs whatsoever, were detained, searched for weapons and photographed, solely because they lived in the barrio. Quite often the cops would delay them for an hour or more, causing them to be late for school or for work. When stopped for the third time, one boy became so aggravated that he refused to answer questions or to be photographed. He waited for just the right moment, then he bolted, yelling back that he was late for work. He didn't get far, though, before a heavy blow knocked him to the ground. He fell face first and immediately tasted a thick pool of warm blood in his mouth. Instinctively he rose to his feet swinging his fists wildly. Two policemen responded by pounding the young boy into the ground. Fortunately for him, the incident occurred within earshot of the *doñas'* house and, within minutes, a crowd of women had gathered in protest. Before the two officers could get the boy into the back of the car, as many as twenty women were blocking them, with more on their way running out of their houses. The boy's mother came between her son and the officers, yelling, "Leave him alone! You have no right to stop him! He was just going to work!"

Then the crowd closed in on the two officers who, caught off guard by the women's aggression, tried in vain to defend themselves as the women stripped them of their equipment and tore at their clothes. As the boy's mother escorted him home to get him cleaned up, the furious mob overpowered and undressed the two bewildered officers. By the time they caught sight of one another through the throng of enraged women, their eyes were filled with panic. A few women made off with their clothes and equipment, while others dismantled the squad car.

They removed everything they could get their hands on: the rifle, radio, emergency equipment, spare tire. They even managed to beat the lights off of the car roof. The officers were left naked, with no place to go but down the street in the hopes that their backup would arrive soon. They were eventually rescued by fellow officers, who brought blankets to conceal them from the procession of euphoric kids that had gathered behind them, whistling and calling out all sorts of dirty innuendo. Wrapped in their blankets, their heads hanging low, the humiliated officers sunk into the back seat of a police car that sped away to the applause of women and children.

Reporters from the *Los Angeles Times*, *La Opinión* and other county newspapers invaded the neighborhood the next morning to interview anyone who witnessed or participated in the disarming and undressing of two police officers. Film crews came from channels 7, 4 and 2, as well as a Spanish channel, and one from Mexico. They set up in front of the little houses, calling through the garden gates:

"Did you see what happened here yesterday?"

"Do you know anyone who was involved in the incident?"

"Why did they do it?"

There was no end to their questions. But no one confessed their involvement, nor would they implicate any of their neighbors.

"I didn't do anything. All that I saw were the two cops, the poor guys, walking down the road, naked and trembling without their guns."

Then the detectives arrived, accompanied by nine officers from the sheriff's department. They parked in front of Felícitas and Paca's house. Micaela was also there. She had been spending so much time with the two ladies that she often stayed the night in a room that they cleared out for her on the second floor, adjacent to the library. They refused to come out to speak with the detectives. Instead, they got to work in the backroom preparing a statement for the barrio.

"We'd like to speak with you!" the detectives shouted from the front door.

"Please, Mrs. Felícitas, Mrs. Paca, come out so we can talk."

For the longest while, no one came out. And while the detectives deliberated over their next move, people began to assemble on the sidewalk and out in the street. Most of them were women, about twenty or so at first. Then more arrived accompanied by other family members, crowding around the officers from the sheriff's department, who began to feel ill at ease amid so many smiling faces and warm bodies that brushed up against them. While the detectives waited at the door beyond the garden gate, the nine officers found themselves completely engulfed by a whirl of people and separated from one another and their cars. Each officer tried to squirm in one direction or another. Their eyes searched for an escape. Disorientated, they stretched out their arms trying to reach the safety of their cars, but it was too late. They were helpless, adrift in a sea of moms, dads, children and grandparents. They felt hands on them, gently pulling at their belts, their buttons, their shoelaces and holsters. In desperation they called out to the detectives, but they too were stupefied by the wall of gazing eyes and smiling faces that appeared out of nowhere.

Then a hush fell over the crowd. The detectives turned back toward the house to see Felícitas emerge in mid-conversation with Micaela, who followed behind. Paca came out next, camera poised with another hanging over her shoulder. She began taking photos of the crowd that pressed up against their fence. The three women stopped at the foot of the stairs where they were met by the anxious detectives.

"Can we please have a moment with you? I don't know what all these people want."

Paca took photos of the detectives. The officers' calls for help from the tangle of community bodies were more audible. Micaela walked past the detectives and approached the crowd. She was impressed by how many had rallied to their cause.

"I don't know why the cops are here!" she yelled out to the crowd. "Do you?"

"No!" was the raucous reply from over three hundred people, most of them women.

"But we do have a message for them, don't we?" She motioned to Felícitas and Paca to close in on the detectives.

"Now hear this! We, women, mothers, grandmothers, wives, daughters, girlfriends and schoolgirls . . . we have taken control of our barrio. And whoever tries to do us harm will have to deal with all of us. We, the women of Geraghty, have a warning for all the homeboys and homegirls . . . for all the violent gangsters out there who cause us to suffer, who hurt us, who terrorize us, who intimidate us, who kill our blessed children. We advise all the pushers and druggies to take their dirty business elsewhere. If we catch you, we'll strip you of everything you own, and we'll kick you out of here ourselves. And if you come around again to sell drugs, it'll cost you, big time! And we advise you, the police, to stop harassing us. We don't need your help, thank you very much. So stop searching our houses, arresting our children and photographing our neighborhood. We don't want you in our barrio because, from now on, we declare that the barrio is ours, and we will be the ones who protect our families and our properties. We will decide the punishment of those who disturb the peace in our community. We do this with love on our side . . . the love of God, the love of family and the love of community. We're not afraid of anyone or of anything, because our weapon against violent criminals is love, and with love on our side we will win this war!" Micaela proclaimed at the top of her lungs.

The crowd replied with a roar of applause, and a round of "Vivas!" Everyone looked around affirming their conviction. Some began to chant parts of Micaela's declaration.

Then Micaela raised her hand to silence the crowd once more.

"Now return to your homes and live in peace, and rest assured that we will fulfill our duty."

Micaela and Felícitas went back into the house while Paca remained outside to film the hundreds of neighbors who had gathered in support of the community. Retreating to their homes, they left nine officers in a daze and, to the surprise of the three detectives, stripped naked. The squad cars had also been stripped clean, missing tires, lights, radios and anything else the community could get their hands on. Only one car was still operational and, without a radio to call for backup, the embarrassed officers huddled inside as best they could. They ended up ripping out the seats and squeezing into the trunk to fit everyone in. Miraculously, the jumble of naked officers and detectives managed to drive off to safety. A few people who stayed behind to watch the sheriffs' antics waved goodbye with big grins, while Paca recorded it all on tape.

On a nearby road, a work crew from the Edison Company had been repairing wires on some rotting posts. They noticed more and more women and children walking past, all headed in the same direction. One of the workmen joined the procession and, just as they were coming up to the commotion in front of the *doñas'* house, the crowd opened up to allow three officers to scramble out naked and disorientated, looking for their cars. The workman remembered that he had a disposable camera in his jacket pocket. He had been taking pictures of his twin boys the night before at their fifth birthday party. He managed to get several good shots of the naked police officers and, after work, he went straight to the newspapers to offer his photos. Two reporters interviewed him and then followed him to where it had all happened. The reporters tried to interview some of the locals, but, to their frustration, no one would say anything. Nevertheless, on the following day, the photos of the naked officers made the front page of the *Herald Examiner*. The reporters confirmed the street names and gave details about the neighborhood where "some of Los Angeles County's deputized community servants" were attacked and dishonored. Reports also appeared on the television news that described the gang-related problems of a troubled neighborhood where the police officers had been humiliated.

"Is it not enough that the sheriffs and L.A. police are there to protect and serve? And the thanks they get is to be attacked and stripped of their clothing and weapons."

The *Daily News* reported that sheriffs had apprehended five pachuco boys from Geraghty and Hazard who were responsible for the attack against the police officers. The suspected gang members had resisted arrest and received "a well-deserved beating." The disgraced officers were interviewed on channel five.

"We have been damaged for life. My identity was taken away by those damn cholos!"

Another officer claimed that his wife could no longer tolerate the shame and ridicule that befell her family.

"My wife took the kids and left me! I'm the laughing stock of my friends and neighbors. Aren't we going to do something about this?" the officer exclaimed in desperation. A few of the officers' children rallied a mob of young men bent on "doing what should have been done a long time ago. It's time we clean up these beaner gangs!" A convoy of about ten cars made its way into East L.A. in search of greasers. Any Mexican boy that fit the gangster description—loose pants, tight T-shirt, a belt pulled up high above the waist—was surrounded, beaten and forced to remove his clothes.

The police and sheriff's departments worked in tandem with the mob, arresting as many as twenty-five Mexicans for public nudity. The raid intensified as more and more vigilantes from different high schools and universities joined in. Now blacks, Asians and even fellow Mexicans were joining the convoy to hunt down the pachuco gangsters, the "beaner gang-bangers." The initial cause of the naked police officers had been long forgotten. And now they attacked any Mexican male who happened to be wearing big pants or a conspicuous shirt. There were calls to 911 demanding police protection coming from every barrio, but, in the morning, the only ones detained were Mexicans. The police's only response to calm the situation was to declare, "Any Latino youth found on the streets after ten p.m., or involved in the rioting, or suspected to be involved in the rioting, will be promptly arrested."

The fact that no attacks were being made against the invading convoys apparently did not factor into the equation.

The situation worsened as the vigilantes set upon any Latino boy out walking at night, beating him savagely, then leaving him naked in the street. The Latino community rallied in protest. Hundreds of mothers flocked to the law offices and detention centers of East L.A. to reclaim their children. On the ten o'clock news Mayor Bowren called for calm as police chiefs announced that they were prolonging the curfew for another night. The public reaction from outside the Latino barrios was positive: "Most of the citizens of this city are delighted with what has been going on."

"All it takes to put a stop to these Mexican gang-bangers is more of the same action as is being done by our law-abiding youth. The cops should learn a lesson from this!"

The news report ended with a declaration from a Latino living in Baldwin Park: "Cholos are scum. They should be eliminated entirely. They deserve to be stripped naked, and the cholas as well."

Throughout these days of unrest, Micaela and the two *doñas* tried to calm the community as best they could, to assist any injured boys, and to help track down the ones who were missing. They helped organize the anxious mothers, to keep peace in the home, explaining their strategy of non-violence to their angry husbands. It was an achievement in itself that not a single death resulted from the violence. Neither Mexicans nor any invading aggressors were killed.

In an interview, Micaela was quoted as saying: "For now the violence against us has ended. But we want everyone to know that if the police invade our neighborhoods to take our children away, they'll suffer the same punishment that we gave their fellow officers. We'll kick them out, naked and disarmed. We repeat that we women have taken control of our neighborhood, and we alone are the judge, jury and executioners of anyone who breaks the law on our streets. We look after ourselves and one another."

This final warning issued by Micaela, with Felícitas and Paca at her side, was televised on national and international broadcasts. As the days passed, the hostilities subsided, but Micaela had captured the attention of the media. Reporters pursued her at every turn, whenever she left the house, at the store, at work in the morning or when she left school in the afternoon. There was always a photographer or reporter nearby. "When are they ever going to leave me alone?" she thought to herself as she quickened her pace on her way to the *doñas'* house. Not surprisingly the joined house of Doña Felícitas and Doña Paca was also receiving unwanted attention.

The police stopped their forays into Geraghty and Hazard, but Micaela was being harassed more than ever. It reached a point where, finally, the school principal called her into the office.

"Micaela, you are an excellent teacher, but a lot of parents are starting to complain. They worry that you're putting their children in danger. And all the reporters that follow you around interrupt our normal routine around here. I'm sorry, Micaela, but we're going to have to remove you from the classroom."

But Micaela wasn't interested in a desk job at the central office and chose to leave the profession altogether. The regional director refused to accept her resignation. For the first few months he managed to grant her sick leave with pay, and then she was granted a leave of absence.

"We really don't want to lose you, Micaela. Please reconsider!" the principal pleaded as he watched Micaela load up her car with the last of her books and teaching supplies before driving off toward Geraghty.

🜸 🜸 🜸

"Micaela, could you please come help me in the morning?" her neighbor Yesenia asked one day in desperation.

Micaela had been helping Yesenia for two weeks when she decided to take Rocío to see the *doñas*. At the door they could hear the sounds of children playing inside. When no one answered, Micaela and Rocío walked in. The two of them stood in the doorway and watched as a young girl positioned the hands of a cardboard clock, a boy quietly drew pictures and an older girl of seven years of age read aloud with Paca at her side.

"Rocío, come on over, sit here while Aurora reads to us."

Rocío sat beside Aurora, who read to her for over an hour. Micaela, Paca and Felícitas found themselves with four children whose mothers could no longer look after them because they had to work. Two mothers went to the *doñas'* house looking for help, and another mother ended up at Micaela's. On the verge of despair, they turned to their community leaders as a last resort.

It began to rain heavily outside. Micaela watched as large puddles formed in the front lawn. Rain water gushed down the street, flowing from the higher plain of the hills. Once in a while, whenever it rained really heavily, it would wash mud and pebbles down the street. Sometimes it would topple houses that balanced precariously on the hillsides. A few years ago it poured for three hours straight. So much rain fell that the earth turned to sludge and came streaming down like chocolate purée, knocking over three houses along the way. There had never been any kind of warning that the houses were at risk of a landslide. All of a sudden they were gone, smashed up against other houses down below. Miraculously, only four people died in the disaster, with another individual still missing, presumably buried in the brown deluge.

"I don't think it's going to rain that much. They said on the radio that it would clear up by tomorrow," Felícitas said.

Micaela turned her attention back to the children. "Look at how well these girls are learning. If only I could get other mothers from the barrio to see children studying and learning like this."

As the rain came down, they watched the four children gathered around Aurora as she read one fairy tale after another.

🐜 🐜 🐜

One morning about a week after the rain, Renata left her house, angry at her mother for insisting that she obey her teachers at school.

Renata was adamant, "I'm not doing it. It's embarrassing. They can kick me out of school. I don't care. I'm not doing it!" Renata yelled as she ran to catch the bus to Belvedere Junior High. Her bus stop was on the same street as the *doñas'* house. She always waved whenever she saw them.

It was a Tuesday when she went into the gym to wait for the teacher. Mrs. Glass insisted that Renata change clothes for gym class just like everyone else, "Girls, get dressed. This is your last chance. If you haven't gotten changed by the time we go out, I'll give you detention."

She was speaking to four girls, including Renata, who refused to get dressed in front of the rest of the class.

"Now get into the locker room, and get ready!" she said in a loud, impatient voice.

After ten minutes all the girls had come out to line up for class, except the four. When Mrs. Glass and three other teachers came back, they went directly over to them, grabbed them by their arms and hauled them into Mrs. Glass' office, which was a chain-linked cage for towel storage. There was another woman inside the cage who looked after the gym equipment.

The rest of the class proceeded to warm up for volleyball drills, led by the team captains who had been picked by Mrs. Glass herself. For about fifteen minutes you could hear screams coming from the cage. When finally they stopped, the doors opened, and Mrs. Glass emerged.

"Girls who don't strip for gym will just have to go naked until they understand that they must cooperate."

As she spoke, the four girls were shoved out of the cage, naked and trembling, for all to see. Renata cried uncontrollably, breaking the silence that fell over the awestruck class.

"We mustn't be ashamed of our bodies," Mrs. Glass continued. "Exercise and cleanliness are next to godliness. I will not have uncooperative girls in my class."

Then she turned to face the cowering naked girls. Renata's convulsive sobbing was interrupted by gasps for air. She was sure that everyone looking at her was laughing at her brown skin and the moles that covered her body: from her small breasts down to her bum and thighs.

"I know that these girls will cooperate from now on. Isn't that right, girls?"

"Yes, Mrs. Glass!" three of the girls replied.

Renata was unable to say anything, as she still struggled to breathe.

"Renata, you can wait naked in the locker room until class is over. Remember, if you want to graduate, you're going to have to strip," Mrs. Glass said triumphantly.

Once the other three had joined the rest of class on the volleyball courts, Mrs. Glass went back to the locker room to find Renata. She threw her clothes onto the floor in front of her.

"I have eighty-some girls out there willing to work with me. You can drop out, for all I care! Get dressed and go to the counselor's office. You've flunked out of this class. And stop sniveling!"

According to Renata's mother, Filomena Pantoja, school, the teachers and the administrators were almost sacred. She had always admired the buildings, the organization, the discipline and, most of all, the books.

"How beautiful to see all the children on their way home from school carrying books," she was explaining to the two *doñas* and Micaela. "And the library, with walls filled with books of every shape and size. Millions of wise words for my Renata to read. That's why when she told me what happened, I just couldn't believe it. But Renata has never lied to me before. I didn't know what to do, which is why I came here. Miss Micaela, you're a teacher. You would know what to do, wouldn't you?"

Filomena appealed to the three women, who were horrified by what they had just heard.

Paca held Renata in her arms on the couch. The girl was crying and repeating that she was never going to go back to school ever again. Felícitas, Micaela and Filomena sat down in the dining room to have coffee and sweet bread. The sun was setting beyond Los Angeles, leaving streaks of purple light in its wake, as darkness crept in over the green hills, the sheltered flower gardens and the warm-lit windows of comfortable little houses. In the fading light, Micaela could always find hope, love and peace for the barrio. She went outside for a walk to collect her thoughts. As she looked at the empty lots and the dilapidated houses that were in desperate need of repair, she thought of how this space could be used to set up a school right in the heart of the barrio.

As the days went by, Micaela discussed this idea with the *doñas,* Filomena and Renata, exploring the possibility of having a learning center constructed on the empty lots, where children and their young mothers could feel protected while getting an education. They imagined an oasis of education and tranquility, something that the neighborhood women had always longed for. They calculated the resources necessary for the women's center and took into account every possible detail.

"Where there's a will, there's a way" is how Micaela explained their endeavor to Rebecca Carter, a reputable lawyer with far-reaching clout, who listened attentively from her office phone in Santa Ana, California.

It was three in the afternoon on a Tuesday when Micaela hung up the phone, hopeful that her dream of a private school for women would be fulfilled. You could see the excitement on her face as she recounted Rebecca Carter's keen interest in the project to the other women who had been waiting with baited breath as Micaela worked out the details on the phone. The *doñas,*

Filomena, Renata, Yesenia, Rocío and other women who had joined the group decided that a little beer and wine was in order. This promising new development called for celebration.

🐜 🐜 🐜

Two cars from rival gangs were parked in front of Costa's store: one from Geraghty and the other from Hazard. The Geraghty boys went into the store for beer. Moments later the Hazard gang came out, with the Geraghty boys close behind them. Words were exchanged as the Hazard gang got into their car. Then, as they began to drive away, the gunfire broke out. Fifteen to twenty gunshots echoed throughout the barrio. Jaramilla Espinoza, who was parked just in front of the Hazard car, was caught in the crossfire. She had come for groceries with her two daughters: her six-year-old, Lidia, and her ten-year-old, Catarina. Jaramilla felt a mosquito whizzing through her hair as the car windows exploded all around them.

Moments later Catarina screamed, "Mommy! Lidia's got no eyes!"

Jaramilla turned to see her daughter bleeding profusely from her face. She frantically clambered over the seats, pressed the limp child against her chest and carried her out of the car. Guns were still firing from both sides, and then the Geraghty car sped away from the scene. By this time Mr. Costa had called 911. People began to appear from every direction, including Micaela, the *doñas* and the other women who had been celebrating that night. They rushed over to help Jaramilla and her girls. No one else was injured but Lidia, who was shot twice and died instantly. The first bullet blew through her eye, and the second one ripped away half of her cranium. What remained of her mutilated face was a mass of hair and blood that coagulated against her mother's sweater.

Jaramilla screamed hysterically. Curses hurled at the gangsters rang out from the crowd of horrified bystanders. Micaela and her friends sheltered Jaramilla and her two daughters, covering them with blankets. As usual, the ambulance and police cars arrived a half hour later. They began to clear a path through the people who were helping Jaramilla and her daughters. At that moment Jaramilla's husband, Mauricio, arrived. When he saw his dead daughter, he yelled at the police not to touch her, then he put his arms around his wife and Catarina. The police officers insisted on seeing the girl. The medical technicians wanted to examine her, but they were unable to wrestle her away from her sobbing family. When two officers finally managed to pull Mauricio away, Jaramilla lowered the girl from her chest onto the ground. The onlookers could see the bits of skull, hair and massive blood clots that covered what remained of Lidia's face. The mother leapt to her feet, screaming, pulling out her hair and tearing at her skin. Micaela and Felícitas did the best they could to hold her back, hugging her tightly and sitting her down on the nearest bench.

All this time Paca had been taking photos of the whole scene. Filomena, Yesenia and other women were asking questions and collecting information about the incident. Before long they had found out the names of the gangsters involved. Once the word was out, an impenetrable silence fell over the crowd. Whoever was being questioned by sheriffs and police officers just listened and said nothing.

Like flies to a rotting corpse, reporters from both English- and Spanish-language stations were drawn to the scene. They claimed their space within the calamity and set up for a live broadcast. Video cameras were heaved up onto shoulders or mounted onto metal tripods.

"We break in twenty minutes!" came a shout from one of the camera trucks.

The cameramen and reporters circulated among the crowd asking questions, but no one wanted to talk to them. No one agreed to be their "eyewitness." No one would cooperate with the media.

"How about you? Did you see anything?" one of the reporters asked Micaela, who responded in a calm and calculated voice.

"You're here to report on how we're killing each other. That's the only thing you came for, to show the blood. In this case there are no sidewalks, so you turn the camera on the blood-stained blankets. You're here to show the victims, the dead girl's hysterical mother. You're here to reveal tragedy inside the barrio and to make heroes of the killers. This slaughter shouldn't be on TV. You take advantage of us. You hope for more killings to keep your eyewitness, action news, *Primer Impacto* fucking jobs. You fuckers create and intensify the anger and the bravado of the gang bangers."

People began to gather behind Micaela to show their support. A younger woman got into the face of a Latino reporter and began her tirade.

"You and the police are as parasitic as the gang bangers, and all of you are the problem. You with your cameras, microphones and helicopters descend on us. You gladly exploit us, you want us to keep killing one another. Secure your job, parasites! You're not here to protect us. You're here to expose us, to keep us corralled in our barrio. You justify the police action against us and warn the outside world not to come in so that the police can have free rein, but that is going to change because we're taking over, we're taking back our neighborhood, our barrio, our homes. And only on our terms do we want parasites like all of you here!"

The reporter and his assistants remained silent through it all, taking in her every word until they caught sight of Lidia's body being loaded into a Salvation funeral hearse. They ran over to the hearse where a detective from the sheriff's department stood watching. From the scene of yet another killing of an innocent victim, caught in the crossfire of gang warfare, the reporter interviewed the detective on live TV.

The interview was interrupted when a group of women stepped in front of the camera, yelling, "Stop the shooting! Stop the killing!"

Upon hearing this, the detective responded, "We'll do everything we can to stop them. You can be sure of that."

Then Micaela stepped in and said to the detective's face, "You won't, but we will, and you can be sure of that."

Then Micaela and her friends escorted Mauricio and his family away from the scene to accompany them in their time of grief.

"You can't take the law into your own hands!" yelled one of the police officers.

"We're going to do the job you can't ever seem to finish!" was the response from the young woman who had confronted the reporter earlier.

"No, you can't! That's our job!" the officer replied.

"Stop the shooting! Stop the shooting! Stop the shooting!" the crowd began to chant as the neighbors assembled behind the Espinoza family, who slowly made their way home.

With the image of hundreds of friends and neighbors from the Geraghty barrio following the grieving family, the reporter recounted Micaela's and the young woman's words to the viewing public: "From what has just transpired here and from what I saw and heard, it appears that these people are serious about taking over and taking back their community."

Two shots from a burst of bullets between rival gangs are what killed Lidia Espinoza. The next day at noon, a certain Martin "Chunky" Gálvez turned himself over to the police, having seen his photo televised all morning long on every local TV station. As far as he was concerned, getting arrested and being watched on TV made him a hero in the eyes of his fellow gangsters. Gálvez had earned respect from his homies, and he knew it, declaring proudly, "I'll do time for my barrio. That's my duty."

Gálvez was the owner of the car the Geraghty gang had left abandoned, riddled with bullet holes. A witness had seen the car on Whittier with three young men inside. As it turned onto Ford St., the witness saw that the driver was steering with one hand and held a gun in the other. He claimed that he saw his face clearly. The driver was Gálvez. The sheriff declared that Gálvez was being accused of murder and was being held in the L.A. Central Jail. But, in reality, the gangsters from Hazard who fired at the Geraghty boys were the ones whose bullets had killed Lidia.

That night Micaela, along with the *doñas,* Filomena, Yesenia and Beatriz (a university student) looked at photos of the perpetrators of the shooting and found out where they lived and the places where they hung out. They talked about the errant bullets that had killed young Lidia, and they shared their observations of how gangs had changed.

"In my day, gangs weren't as violent," Felícitas said.

"I don't ever remember so much violence, so many guns," Paca added as she loaded another film cartridge into her Leica camera.

"Now gangsters are drug dealers who wage war not to defend their barrio or their homies, but to protect their share in the market, their little corner for selling drugs," Beatriz explained.

"You're right, Beatriz," Micaela affirmed. "But now there's an additional destructive force that entices them, that makes them feel like heroes, like they're living the dream of seeing their face on the big screen. It's the media that broadcast live images of these murderers as they speed off in a getaway, or of the police who've been shot, or dead bodies under a yellow plastic tarp. In the eyes of young children, potential new gang members, these murderers are like mythical Titans, war heroes from the ghetto. The feeling of being most wanted, like the bad guy in an action movie, that intense moment of being recognized by the eyes of the world, that's the psychological drug that makes them pull out a gun and shoot in all directions, killing anyone in their sight. The flashing lights and frenzied images hold the gaze of impressionable children, structuring the mentality of future 'pee wees,' 'little troopers,' or five-year-old 'tinies' who hold a heavy hand gun on their laps on their way to a drive-by, or a 'mission,' or a swarming, on a wild and crazy adventure to take revenge against an enemy gang. But now, girls, we're going to be the ones doing the swarming. We'll track down these homies and home girls, their houses and their families until they stop the shooting." Micaela looked around. The women had been listening to her every word, surrounded by photos on every wall in Paca's studio, photos that housed the history of the barrio.

With her scrapbook of newspaper clippings opened in front of her, Felícitas read one of the statements issued by a gangster in an interview.

"The only thing we can do is build our own little nation. We know that we have complete control of our community. It's like we're making our stand. . . . We're all brothers and nobody fucks with us. We take pride in our little nation and if any intruders enter, we feel our community is being threatened. The only way is with violence. And nobody, not even our own, can stand in the way of protecting our little nation."

"Maybe so. But now we're going to take control of our neighborhood, of our streets, so that our sons and daughters can live without fear. I'm fed up already with being a woman living in constant fear," Filomena responded.

"Drugs make them crazy. They'd sell their own sisters or girlfriends for drugs. Drugs dehumanize them. Addicts aren't even human beings anymore. The poor bastards have turned into perverse deformities that are better off dead," Yesenia added, surprised by her own words.

"Guns are as bad as the drugs. The more guns there are in the neighborhood, the more fall into the hands of gangsters, resulting in more killings and more acts of vengeance. As soon as guns enter the equation, the neighborhood is broken up into indistinguishable pockets of violence where fear allows gangs to operate unchallenged," Beatriz interjected.

"All they care about is their reputation. They want to be heroes, crazy motha-fuckers, fearless *vatos locos* who protect the honor of their barrio and their gang at all costs. They never back away from anything. They'd rather die. And if any of this gets on TV, so much the better. If the shooting attracts media attention, the helicopters that hover over the crime scene, or if the police shoot at them in a high-speed chase, or kill them right there in front of the cameras, that's how you die with honor. That's how you show all the other homies the right way to go. It's all one big live repugnant theater that makes me sick," Felícitas retorted.

"When it happened, young Lidia was talking about how she wanted her fifteenth birthday celebration. They say she was describing her party as if it were her last, when the bullets struck and blew through her face," Paca said as she raised her camera to take a few photos of her friends.

"Do you really think that they'll listen to us? A bunch of women?" Beatriz asked doubtfully.

"You still don't know what the women of this barrio are capable of," Felícitas replied confidently. "They've rallied behind us before. You don't know this, Beatriz, because you weren't there." Yesenia looked at Felícitas as Paca and Micaela rose to stand beside her.

"What can a bunch of women do? We can decide our own future, that's what we can do. We can plan and build our own community. Our actions are simple, our cause is just and our mission is sacred," Micaela replied firmly.

It was past midnight. Micaela, looking out the window, decided that it was time to go home. First Micaela, then Beatriz, followed by Filomena and Yesenia, exited the *doñas'* house and stopped a moment at the bottom of the front stairs to contemplate each other's face in the dim starlight. Then each woman followed her own path home.

☙ ☙ ☙

It was three in the morning when, led by Micaela and the *doñas,* more than a hundred women were quietly making their way from the *doñas'* headquarters on Beulah St., toward Geraghty. They turned right off of Beulah, then, before reaching Botswick St., they stopped in front of an old wooden house that was completely dark inside. Using the same methods as the police, they knocked down the front door using a sledge hammer, and then they turned on all the lights as they rushed in to look for Uriel and Neto Vargas, the two Geraghty homies who were in the gunfight with the Hazard gang. Most of the houses on Geraghty were small wooden structures pushed up against each other. Some were sunk down below street level, supporting other houses that were built behind them. Others hung on terraces that were built into the hillside. All of the houses in these ancient heights—on Stringer Street, Loats, Swiggins, Robinson, Botswick and Beulah—were constructed one on top of the other, forming a pyramid of little dwellings for families that lived so close together they could feel each other's warmth, their happiness, their anger and the beating of their hearts. Whenever there was an emotional upheaval, as when Lidia was killed, the residents of City Terrace, Hazard and Geraghty joined as one body with a common voice lamenting the sadness. On these hills, teeming with primeval life, the group of women closed in on Uriel and Neto who, fast asleep, were caught completely off guard by the crashing door and the ensuing home invasion. Terrified, they jumped out of bed, but it was too late. The women had already begun removing their clothes.

"What are you doing to my boys?" the father yelled.

"Leave them alone! They're good boys! They didn't do anything!" their mother, Estela, pleaded.

"Because of these boys an innocent little girl was killed," Felícitas responded.

As the women pinned down Uriel and Neto and removed their clothes, they instructed them to start praying and to beg for forgiveness. By now the group had grown to close to three hundred women who waited eagerly for word from Micaela and the *doñas* who had led the charge.

"What are you going to do to my boys? Where are the police?" Estela cried, fearful of the crowd of women who swelled inside her little home. Then the parents heard their boys praying.

"What are you doing to them?" Estela pleaded once again.

"We are here to carry out God's justice. Like you, Estela, we women love our boys, but we can no longer tolerate the killing of innocent children. Our love is God's love, and with God's love we are banishing Uriel and Neto. Just look at how the homies and the gangsters think they can control the neighborhood, committing crimes at will because they know that the police won't do anything about it, and because they think the community is too afraid to defend itself. Well, in memory of

Lidia's death, and of other innocent victims who died from a stray bullet, we now declare this land to be sacred. And from now on, we women will perform God's justice, and we don't want your sons living among us any longer. They are hereby banished from these sacred hills. Your boys aren't going to die, but they are not allowed to come back to this neighborhood until they change their ways. And if they do come back, it will cost them."

Micaela held her gaze on the parents as Uriel and Neto were escorted from their home, naked and ashamed, to disappear behind the mass of women. For an instant the boys caught sight of their parents for the last time. Neto, the youngest, was crying. Uriel, struggling to see through the veil of long dark hair, cried out for his mother. Within a few minutes his cries fell silent, replaced by the sound of footsteps as hundreds of women returned to their homes.

On the following night, around four o'clock in the morning, the same crowd of about three hundred women swarmed into Melven Triquitas's house, one of the Hazard homies. The *doñas* had learned that the other two had run off as soon as they heard about Uriel and Neto. Word travels quickly through the barrio, and when the women stopped in front of Melven's house, his parents, Mario and Adela, were ready to confront them, knocking one of the lead women onto her back before she could utter a word.

"Get the fuck out of here, you meddling old bitches! My son didn't do anything, so leave us the fuck alone!" The father tried to hit another woman, but this time she ducked out of the way. He was instantly smothered by some twenty women who latched on to him, wrapping themselves around his neck, torso, arms and legs. He called out to his wife, Adela, who, stepping aside from the surge of women, cried out, "Where are you? Are you all right?"

Inside, Melven held up an ax handle to defend himself against the angelic apparitions that stormed into his bedroom. Adela offered no resistance, and she had no choice but to allow the women to apprehend her son. Melven protested, insisting that he hadn't killed the girl, yet the throng of women drew closer and closer until they pressed him up against the wall. Then they proceeded to remove what little clothing he had been wearing in bed. Melven slid to the floor where he wriggled in vain. When the women opened a space in front of him, he looked wild and furious, but his fury soon gave way to help-lessness. Naked, on his knees, Melven realized that there was no escape. He watched as Micaela spoke with his mother. A few minutes later, another group of women came into his room to take him away.

"Don't you ever come back here again. If you return without changing your ways, you'll suffer the consequences. From this day onward, you are banished." Micaela pronounced the sen-tence while Paca filmed the exile of Melven, the homeboy.

With God's work accomplished, the crowd dispersed and returned home, while others dragged Melven away from the house. Shivering from cold and fear, he had to stop and pee right in the middle of the lawn. The warm mist of urine hung over the cool wet grass as the last cars disappeared down the deserted winding streets of Geraghty.

🐜 🐜 🐜

It was in San Diego, beneath an underpass in Chicano Park, that two officers found a young man wandering naked and dis-oriented. When he saw the police he became frightened and tried to cover himself with his arms and hands. Melven did not run. He just put his hands up and said, "I'm cold." As for Uriel and Neto, they were never heard from again. Some said that they had gone to live with relatives in Moreno Valley.

The police came once again to investigate. A police captain phoned Micaela and the *doñas* in advance to inform them that as many as twenty-five officers would be showing up to carry out the investigation. He made it clear that he didn't want any problems and he was prepared to respond accordingly should he need to protect his officers.

"We just want to ask a few questions. We want to see the houses where three boys disappeared."

Micaela wouldn't say yes or no. She just wished him a good day and hung up the phone. People in the community had grown accustomed to the police interrogation rituals, which always ended with someone being detained for further questioning. Now it was worse because INS agents, the *migra,* were accompanying the police, on the lookout for illegal aliens. Nothing had changed: for decades the police had always looked at Mexicans as suspects and their barrios as a criminal underworld. When they needed a scapegoat, they stormed in and apprehended two or three boys. The neighborhood residents had grown distrustful of the police, seeing them more as an army of occupation than as public servants. The squad cars patrolled the streets to ensure that Mexicans were staying within a limited area, to keep them in the barrio, to confine them to their own territory. The police were present, not to keep the peace but to impose borders. And now the war between the gangs and the police had transformed the police into nothing less than another violent gang. That's how residents saw the police: just more violent young men hunting down enemy gangs to shoot at them, to kill them, and through blood and tears, to create more work for themselves. This time, just like every other time, they showed up with the same questions.

"Who kidnapped Uriel, Neto and Melven?"

"The community women did, officer."

"Who stripped Melven Trinquitas?"

"The women from Geraghty, officer."

That afternoon the police learned absolutely nothing. By remaining silent, the community, the women in particular, grew stronger. When they passed each other on the street, they smiled secretively and with a conscience free of fear or guilt, united by a feeling of moral solidarity.

᠅ ᠅ ᠅

At an old folk's home filled with World War II veterans, a tattered American flag snapped and curled in a fresh breeze that blew the smog out of the L.A. basin, offering Geraghty residents an infinitely clear blue sky. In City Terrace, some of the houses that faced Los Angeles had an unobstructed view of downtown. Agueda Josefina Salcedo opened her front door to receive Micaela, the *doñas* and a few of their associates. Agueda was acquainted with all of them except Beatriz, the young university student. When she came up to the house she was immediately struck by the panoramic view, and she paused at the door to contemplate the vista that stretched as far as Santa Monica.

"Please come in," her hostess said. "And do make yourself at home."

The visitors were all moved by the geographic perspective and architectural beauty of Los Angeles. "We are the angels of Los Angeles," Beatriz whispered softly. The women felt as though they somehow embodied the city. Adding to her first impression, Beatriz was greeted by a prism of colors: Agueda's multi-toned sweater, blouse and layered skirt.

"*De colores,* that's me. And the brighter the better," Agueda said in a singsong voice and broad smile.

She stood five feet, four inches tall, with short brown hair. She always wore colorful baggy sweaters. She had the habit of keeping her hands in her pockets and her arms tucked up against her sides as if she were hiding something underneath that bright layer of wool. When she was among other women she would take off her sweater, revealing an enormous bust that bounced and swayed with her every movement.

It never ceased to surprise even her closest friends just how buxom she was. Whenever Agueda went to the kitchen to fetch coffee or tea, her friends would invariably make some sort of comment.

"How on earth does the poor woman manage with those massive jugs?" Filomena gasped.

"Nowadays you can get a breast reduction," Beatriz added.

"Yeah, but for a price, and she barely makes enough to get by on."

"I can't imagine why she doesn't have a man out there working for her."

"She's got big enough boobs for two men!"

They all laughed.

"And what does that have to do with anything? Look what I've got!" Yesenia interrupted as she pulled up her shirt to reveal a flat chest dotted by two plum-colored nipples. "I've got nothing, but I've been with enough men to form a platoon!"

After a good laugh the women began unfolding metal chairs and placing them around a long table in the middle of the living room.

"I just love this house," Jaramilla said to Adela.

For both women it was their first time visiting Agueda. Paca took photos of her friends, of the walls and of the rooms throughout the house. Each room was painted a different color. The ceiling contrasted with the colorful walls which, in turn, contrasted with the wooden floors that were painted yellow the length of the house. Then it dawned on Jaramilla that she had just been speaking with the woman whose son had killed her daughter, Lidia. Then she looked at her again, and this time she wanted to rip out her heart for giving birth to the fucking monster!

Adela's spirit was broken. She was defeated by the sadness of having lost a child of her own. But her grief was more gradual as she had lost her son, Melven, to gang life. When he was only ten years old he was brought home one night by police officers who warned her not to let him hang out with the Hazard homeboys. If he got any further involved with gangs, he would end up in juvenile detention. Melven started drinking and shooting up. Then he dropped out of school. At age thirteen Melven found himself one night posing defiantly outside his house. With his shirt off he displayed the image of the Virgin tattooed on each arm, "Hazard" written across his chest and a mock teardrop below his left eye.

"Kill me, you motherfuckers!" he yelled at the police who were quickly moving in on him. They grabbed him, beat him and took him away without so much as a word to Adela. From that day on Melven would do time in more than twelve different California penitentiaries and detention centers. He would become one of the most notorious gangsters known throughout Los Angeles and the most feared and loathed among rival gangs around Hazard and Geraghty. He was a lost boy, a drug addict, a rapist and a violent murderer who was loved and cared for by his devoted mother, Adela. Her life had become an eternal agony that tore at her very soul as she helplessly watched the moral putrefaction of her only son.

Micaela drew near and put her arm around Jaramilla, who was on the verge of saying or doing something. Intuitively, Micaela stepped in. What she saw in Jaramilla's eyes may have been a yearning for Lidia or a desperate confusion between hatred and depression directed at both Adela and herself.

"Jaramilla, come see the altars that Agueda makes." Micaela took her by the arm and pulled her over to the long table that was now covered with paints, dyed paper, blocks and slabs of wood, crepe paper, portraits and candles.

"These are the materials that she starts with to make her altars. And that's why we're here. She's going to show us how to make altars the traditional way," Micaela explained.

She paused for a moment and imagined dim lights glowing through the windows of little Geraghty houses. In the light she saw the Virgin resting on a mattress laid out on a wooden floor. She was a thirty-year-old woman stretched out on the mattress, with long brown hair down to her hips. Her face was round and peaceful, she had full red lips, a small mouth underneath a sculpted nose and eyes the color of coffee. Her neck was long and muscular. Her skin and her ribs, the bones in her chest had all been removed. It was as if a surgeon had traced an incision around her entire torso and removed the skin and bones to reveal the inner organs from her throat down to her vagina. Her organs palpitated for the whole world to see. Each organ throbbed with life, even her heart which had been cut open to expose the inner workings that pulsed and recoiled as the woman slept calmly. For an instant, this was the image that she saw in the Virgin of Guadalupe altars that covered the wall in front of her.

Micaela pondered these brightly colored altars and thought of Agueda as a rare talent, a real master of a craft that has been all but forgotten by Mexican immigrants. As she worked, Agueda explained how she was preparing the materials and piecing them together. She also explained how she learned the tradition in the motherland. It was customary to construct an altar for special events like weddings, baptisms and always whenever someone died. Agueda modified her altars to suit the deceased. If it were a man of some importance in the community, she would mount a public display so that people could pay their respects to him and his family. Were it a mother, she would make a more delicate altar to reflect the family's love. If it were an innocent child, she would surround the altar with little angels and use the child's favorite colors. For a wake, people would usually put the altar in the living room, where it would remain for the next nine days of prayer following the burial. Graced by the familiar presence of the Virgin of Guadalupe, the prayers were destined to accompany the soul as it ascended to heaven. The night of the wake, people would bring fresh fruit, flowers and objects that represented the departed soul's favorite things in life. Here in the barrio, where the only constant is change, Agueda Josefina Salcedo worked to preserve the sacred tradition of making altars.

"I don't want to just see them in museums and at religious festivals. Altars belong in every home for every family in the barrio. Everyone should maintain their own altar, a place to go for quiet reflection, or to speak freely to our Lady, and to ask the Lord for His blessing."

Agueda had learned to make altars at the age of five. She learned by watching her mother who had learned the craft from Agueda's grandmother who, in turn, had learned from her great-grandmother, and so forth. Agueda was, in fact, a link in a long chain of artists who had preserved a tradition dating back to the colonial era.

"First you need to feel the cause itself, the very reason why you need to build an altar. You need to immerse yourself in the emotion of the cause. You need to see the faces of the people affected. Your heart needs to beat with their hearts, as one. Only in this way will you discover the true meaning of the altar and the shape and image that it should take. Once you have captured this image in your mind, you can begin working towards it, always sensitive to the beating of the hearts of the people who are affected by it, so that they can participate in the creative process. In the end you will not even recognize the image that had come to you originally, but they will tell you that it's their image, and you will recognize this in their smiles and in their tears of joy, the personal release that comes to each individual and the collective relief experienced by the family and the community. This will be your apotheosis as an artist. In this way you will be guided when cutting the crepe and tissue paper in the form of religious figures, candles, birds and, most of all, flowers. Sometimes a single altar may be adorned with more than a thousand flowers. Be happy doing this work for your fellow man, and for God," Agueda concluded as she maneuvered her breasts out of the way of her busy hands.

She began to cut, fold and apply glue to pieces of paper. Very carefully she affixed each piece, directing the other women to follow along.

"A work of art is more than a simple arrangement of pieces. And what we are doing transcends art."

Agueda motioned to the altars that were placed all around the room, some on tables, others on walls, and larger ones which rose from the floor to the ceiling.

"Altars," Agueda continued, "represent the lives of people who have walked these roads in other times. They are the lives of our ancestors. When I create an altar, I feel like I'm in the presence of my mother and my grandmother."

Paca took more photos. Micaela served coffee and hot chocolate while the guests worked, paying close attention to Agueda as she explained the meaning of altars and demonstrated how to cut out the intricate images.

"I like making altars because I feel like they keep me company," Agueda said, making a huge effort to lift her body and get to her feet.

Micaela studied the altars, each one with an image of the Virgin, erected in honor of the departed. She thought of all the children who had died from gang violence, from drugs or from physical abuse, and imagined their images on altars of their own. Altars could also help us remember the face of innocence. "And, why not have altars for the living?" Micaela thought to herself, "for children who excel in school, for people who do good deeds for the community, for the poor who work hard to see their children get ahead in life?" Deep in thought, she turned her gaze to the array of tools and materials on the table where the women were all working. She noticed a pile of scissors of all shapes and sizes.

"You know what?" Micaela said as she grabbed a pair of scissors and examined them closely. "We should always carry a pair of these. Scissors will be our weapon against gangsters and the police. We'll take back our neighborhood armed with scissors alone."

The weather worsened. It rained hard for an entire day, followed by a few days of sunshine and clear blue skies. It was neither hot nor cold outside, but the climate was perfect for creative and collective initiatives. The women were still thinking about their day at Agueda's house and how they should develop and carry out some sort of innovative communal action. On that day they listened to Micaela urge them to keep up the fight and to reclaim their neighborhood. Only a small percentage of these kids were gangsters, and yet they brought so much harm to so many. Most other kids were interested in doing well at school and avoiding confrontations with gangs.

"The homies that are in these gangs are kids that won't be easy to save. Many of them have tasted the glory of going to jail. Many of them are institutionalized souls who have lost all fear of the system—that is, the police and prison. The worst that can happen to them is to be killed, and they're not even afraid of that. From the time that they're just little kids they begin to see the prison system like a school, a home even, because there they have everything they need. They're converted by the authorities into beings that are dependent on the very system that's supposed to deter them from criminal life. But this process of institutionalizing young kids from the barrio guarantees thousands, if not millions of jobs, and billions of dollars. Jobs and money, they're both related in one way or another to the production and preservation of crime and criminal culture. To be incarcerated earns them respect among their peers, and they enjoy the publicity that they receive from the papers, the radio and TV. It satisfies their hunger for recognition and an identity. After killing someone, they love seeing their names in the headlines. Once they make it to public enemy number one, they're lost for good to the rush of their fleeting notoriety."

Micaela analyzed the situation in her neighborhood and then described a corresponding plan of action. That afternoon Micaela, Felícitas and Paca finalized the idea of building a school for the neighborhood kids that would be run entirely by women. Before leaving they came to the agreement that they would form the Women's Scissor Federation, dedicated to the salvation of women and children who suffer abuse, intimidation and violence from gangs, the police and society's parasitic media. Their Federation would join the ranks of other groups dedicated to improving their respective communities, such as the Peace in the Barrio Committee and the Mother's Alliance for Child Protection.

⚔ ⚔ ⚔

Six months had passed since the declaration of the Women's Scissor Federation. The house of the two *doñas* had been converted into an educational center and safe house for women and children from the barrio. Women came to Micaela, Felícitas and Paca for guidance. Those who became members of the Federation saw the benefits of at least psychological prosperity, gaining confidence from their growing numbers. They soon realized that gangs tended to avoid neighborhoods where residents were organized against criminal activity and, in this case, against the ensuing police and media invasions that came with it.

After years of atrocities stemming from gang and domestic violence, the Federation decided to organize, analyze and take action. They realized that the primary causes of their despair were poverty, lack of education, lack of job training and inadequate parenting. Only four to ten percent of kids from the barrio were affiliated with gangs, and yet they caused so much suffering for so many women.

The Center confronted these problems by providing childcare so that mothers could work and go back to school. It offered leadership training, and tutor and counselor training for junior high and high school students. They organized a committee for carrying out justice in the barrio. Instead of just maintaining the peace by talking with gangsters to try to prevent more violence, the members of this committee went much further. Fed up with talking to homies and homegirls, the Federation opted to fight fire with fire. Micaela and the women from the Federation were prepared to pull out their scissors to bring justice to the barrio and keep the peace. Over time, the word spread of their efforts, and more and more women came to the Federation to offer donations and help. Their numbers grew stronger each day.

One morning some reporters showed up with a group of politicians who wanted to have their photo taken with women from the Federation. At the same time, an actor all dressed in black arrived. He had played the same exaggerated Latino gangster role so many times that he became a hero. Flanked by his five bodyguards and three secretaries, the very famous Ego Thespis had entered the scene. He greeted the politicians and everyone else who had come to gather in front of the *doñas'* house. For the reporters and television crews it was turning out to be the perfect spectacle.

The dignitaries did not have to wait long. Micaela, Felícitas and Paca, taking photos as always, emerged from the house to greet them. They were followed by other women and their children and a few of the volunteers.

"There's nothing here for you, so move it along and leave these good women alone," Micaela announced.

"We don't want your help, your allegiance and much less your publicity," another women affirmed.

The actor, proud and powerful, stepped up in front of the women and cleared his throat. "I've come to offer my help, to offer you funding and to help you organize. Let me come in and show you how I can make you all famous. We can make a movie about you!" he proposed enthusiastically.

Jaramilla, whose girl Lidia had been blown away by gangster gunfire, spoke out in reply: "You, sir, are the worst of all. You're nothing but a fake, a pachuco who made millions off the misery and the suffering of your own people. You've glorified murderous gangsters, the parasites that destroy our community. Go to hell, you phony wanna-be!"

Jaramilla straightened up, standing firm in defiance of Ego Thespis, the politicians and the reporters. Just because she had always been poor and looked down on, she was not going to remain silent. Her opinion mattered, she thought to herself as she heard the applause and whistles behind her.

When a photographer began taking photos of Jaramilla, Micaela jumped in. "No! We don't allow photos!"

Four women grabbed the photographer and wrestled with him long enough to remove the film from his camera.

"We don't want photos, video clips or interviews! We're tired of your damn helicopters invading our private space. What good to us is all your commercial attention. You and the police have done us a serious disservice. We don't want you to serve us anymore!"

The onlookers who had turned up to witness the excitement began to cheer, sing and slowly push the reporters and politicians back to their cars. With their scissors in hand, the Federation women managed to catch Ego Thespis by surprise, separating him from his embarrassed body guards. Escorting him down the street, they began to open and close their scissors to the beat of their accelerating march until Ego Thespis broke free and made a run for it, terrified as if he'd seen his own ghost.

🐜 🐜 🐜

A month after the visit from the politicians, the press and Ego Thespis, Micaela looked around but could find none of them at the funeral mass for yet another fallen homeboy from the barrio. This time it was the notorious Ricky "Chivo" Rodríguez, a crazy cholo from Geraghty that the Ford Flats gang had tried to kill on more than one occasion. This time they got him in a drive-by just as he was coming out of church. As El Chivo was crossing himself with the last Person of the Trinity and of his life, a .45-calibre bullet blew through the back of his neck. El Chivo fell with his mouth open halfway through a sigh and his eyes wide open toward the sky. Micaela remembered that it took half an hour before the paramedics finally arrived to attend to the boy who lay dying, and that no politician came to visit the boy's family, and that no actor like Ego Thespis came to propose making a movie about the boy's life, and that no Latino reporter came to offer live coverage, and that only a couple of cops came with the hearse to collect El Chivo's body. As always, the neighborhood women took up a collection for the burial, and for the wake an altar was constructed by Doña Agueda in memory of the barrio's latest victim.

A week after El Chivo was buried in Calvary Cemetery, Danny "Little M" Quintillas was shot when he was walking along César Chávez Boulevard with his girlfriend, Carmen Martínez. Though Danny received five bullet wounds, it was Carmen who died from the attack, as she was shot through the head. Danny spent a week in the hospital, itching to avenge Carmen's death. As soon as he was released, he took a few hits of heroin, got hold of a gun and then cruised into Hazard on a search-and-destroy mission. The sun was setting over the Pacific and, under the darkening red sky, Danny, with three of his homies from Maravillas, parked in front of the Reinosa house and waited. When they finally opened fire on the Hazard boys, Gloria Reinosa jumped with fear as the bullets blasted through her window. The terror on her face was the last thing two-year-old Tomás would ever see before he lay lifeless in his mother's arms.

As Tomás Reinosa lay in his little casket lined with white satin and lace, Micaela and a militia of Scissor Federation women took their positions, surrounding the garage in back of Danny "Little M" Quintillas's house. Danny and his homies were smoking pot and having some fun with a crazy homegirl who was making the rounds with her shirt off. Though they were caught completely off guard, the boys managed to fire three shots before they were slammed to the floor by the onrush. Two women were wounded by the gunfire, and were taken for treatment at a private clinic.

Stoned, Danny and his homies lay pinned to the floor as the women worked at cutting away their clothes. One woman loomed ominously overhead with a pair of surgical scissors. The girl had her shirt put back on and, with her arms held behind her back, she was forced to watch the procedure, to bear witness to the consequences of living the *vida loca*. The women prayed the rosary as Danny erupted into convulsive screams, and their prayers grew louder and louder to absorb his cries. Danny's punishment for killing young Tomás Reinosa had begun.

When finally they dragged him from the garage to pull him into a car, his frantic mother was trying to claw her way through the women, "Leave my boy alone! Please, let him go, he didn't do anything!"

At the precise moment when they dumped Danny, bleeding profusely from between his legs to the horror of his three homies, on a side street near the county hospital, Gloria Reinosa was pulling out her hair and ripping at her own clothes in front of Tomás' casket.

"I don't want to live anymore!" she cried. "I don't care anymore! Please God, take me from this hell so I can be with Tomás!"

Beatriz leaned down in front of Danny and looked directly into the dull glaze of his blood-shot eyes.

"Give thanks to God that we have spared your life. Don't ever come back to this neighborhood again without changing your ways, because the penalty will be even worse next time, for you, your homies and everyone who knows you. You can tell your gangster friends that the Women's Scissor Federation now controls this barrio. I'm warning you out of love, my brother, with the love of Jesus Christ. Now drag your sorry ass over to the hospital because from now on your life is in your own hands."

Beatriz helped him stagger to his feet and passed him over to his homies. The women watched as four naked young men slowly made their way under the bright lights of the emergency ward. One of them was cradling his penis and blood-soaked scrotum from where the women had cut out his testicles.

֎ ֎ ֎

On the second floor of the *doñas'* house, Micaela was taking a shower and looking out the small window at the Geraghty streets below. Large palm trees swayed their droopy branches in a playful evening breeze. Two teenage girls were tentatively making their way toward the house. They had spoken with Micaela a couple of weeks earlier, but they stopped short under a tree. One of them was looking up contemplating the gentle sway of the palms. Then she looked toward the house and nudged her friend, urging her on. The short distance to the front gate seemed like miles to Reina, but Carmen finally took her by the arm and ushered her across the street slowly and painfully, for Reina was badly bruised from the beating she had just received from her parents.

"You're lucky the ol' lady took the belt away from him. He was going to kill you this time," Carmen said as she helped her friend hobble along.

"First he took my money away, then he started throwing me around. He thinks I'm fuckin' every homeboy in town."

"Now you're out on the street, babe. So where are we supposed to sleep?" Carmen grumbled.

"What the fuck, Carmen! Your stepfather beats your *chola* ass, too. First he fucks your mama whenever she's stoned, then he beats you around trying to get into your pants. That's why you came runnin' to my house."

"So my mother's a druggie. I don't want to hear about it, okay bitch? Now come on, I hear these old ladies are real nice. It's just a few more steps," Carmen replied, trying to get her friend through the gate.

"I can't. Just wait. I can't fuckin' breathe!"

Micaela was getting dressed when she heard the *doñas* yelling for help. She ran down to the front lawn where she found Felícitas and Carmen dragging Reina to the front steps. Paca was clicking away with her camera.

"Paca, give the damn camera a rest and help us get this girl into the house!" Micaela exclaimed.

Carmen and Reina had shown up, not because they wanted to but because they were desperate. They had no home, no parental care and no friends who could help them. They didn't want to ask the homeboys for help because, if they did, a few days later they'd have to pay protection fees with their bodies.

As El Chivo told all the dumb-ass homegirls who clung to him from either fear or addiction, "It's time to pay for your family care, you little whores. I'm your daddy and remember that Daddy tells you what to do and when to do it."

Carmen and Reina refused to become slaves for some horny gangster, much less for a little nation homeboy. Nor could they turn to other homegirls, because they were no longer welcomed among them. Far too often Carmen and Reina had been accused of stealing drugs or money whenever they hooked up with other girls. They were called "dirty little thieves," "useless whores," "crazy bitches." They had no choice but to seek help from the Women's Scissor Federation. The news had spread through the barrio that these women helped anyone seeking refuge from gangs. And they weren't doing it for a documentary, or to be in the news, or so that an actor like Ego Thespis would make a movie about them. Their efforts to support the community were for real. These women had consistently refused help from the police, church groups, reporters and celebrities because they felt that these entities were making the most of gang activity in the same way that gangs were exploiting communities. Carmen and Reina had had enough. They were ready to hang with women who lived up to their words, taking action instead of just talking about it. Though they didn't know it yet, these girls would physically confront gangsters, cops, reporters and anyone else who harmed the barrio in some way. This would be their destiny.

That night, Grayson Ramírez-Yim entered the second-floor bedroom of the Federation Center to attend to the wounded girl. The doctor who, like Paca, was also a photographer, strongly recommended that Reina go to a hospital because her ribs were broken, severely enough to leave abrasions on her lungs. Reina refused at first, but after an hour she was screaming from the intensifying pain. They took her to the county hospital. Then, after a week, she returned to her new home.

🐜 🐜 🐜

Carmen had spent the week living at the Center, helping out in the daycare where mothers would leave their children in the morning so they could go off to work. The women who volunteered their time at the daycare were the grandmothers, the widows and spinsters who would otherwise spend the day at home. Micaela and the *doñas* had convinced them to become members of the Federation and to participate any way they could. As many as thirty women had since come to offer their time, their love and their valuable experience at the daycare.

The Federation was also offering courses for girls like Carmen and Reina who had quit school. There were currently fourteen girls studying at the Center, receiving their education from two retired school teachers: Mrs. Kochart and Mrs. Marbel. Having lived in Geraghty for over forty years and, as good friends of the *doñas,* they were happy to develop a school curriculum for the Center.

Micaela, Felícitas, Filomena, Yesenia and Jaramilla were all sitting out on the small balcony of the house, resting at the end of another long day. Looking west toward the Pacific, they were counting the planes that landed at LAX, their jet streams crossing a purple and orange sky, dusted with crimson clouds at twilight. Just inside the door, Paca was organizing photos that she had just developed, arranging them on the floor and studying each one carefully while Beatriz, Adela, Agueda and Carmen offered their comments as they looked over her shoulder. Paca had taken down at least fifty photos from the walls to replace them with new ones. When Adela spied her Melven among the photos on the floor, she caught her breath and began to weep with the indelible image of his smiling face etched in her memory. Adela grabbed the photo and, holding it against her chest, she moved to the corner where she could cry in what little privacy the room had to offer. The women around her lowered their voices as they continued to help Paca with her latest project.

"Let's put these ones up here," Beatriz suggested.

The women worked away at selecting the best photos to go up on the wall when, all of a sudden, Adela turned and burst out, "Shut up! You stupid bitches! Can't you see that I'm crying for my son? Don't you have any compassion?"

The women from outside on the balcony squeezed into the room, led by Jaramilla, who had overheard Adela's protest.

"Compassion? You ungrateful bitch. That dirty bastard killed my Lidia!" was Jaramilla's response.

Adela rose to her feet and spoke slow deliberate words to Jaramilla: "Go . . . to . . . Hell."

"Hell is where I'll send you, you stupid whore! Now shut up or . . . "

Before Jaramilla could finish, Adela was on top of her with fists full of hair. The two women shrieked as they punched and kicked at each other rolling around on the floor. They bit each other, they raked and clawed at one another's face and eyes. They ripped at each other's clothes, digging their nails deeply into each other's skin. Blood and tears covered their faces and the crumpled photos on the floor that portrayed a barrio's violence: angry crowds, homeboys in handcuffs, blood-drenched sidewalks, body bags, funeral wakes, screams of agony, terror and despair. The other women tried to separate them, but Adela and Jaramilla were intent on killing one another. The intervening women managed to get hold of their hands, but the two foes just kicked more furiously. Finally they dragged each woman by the hair into a separate room after a lengthy struggle.

Felícitas and Micaela attended to Adela who, upon making eye contact with Micaela, burst into convulsive tears, interrupted by threats of suicide, "I can't do this anymore . . . I want to die!"

Adela trembled from a chill and was soaked with sweat. Her friends got her some dry clothes and helped her get dressed. A couple of hours later it became apparent that she needed medical care. Adela had become disorientated and was incoherent. When she soiled herself, the women got organized, cleaned her up and took both injured women to the hospital.

Jaramilla, accompanied by Carmen, Reina and Agueda, sat calmly, listening to Adela cry from the room across the hall. It was ten o'clock when Dr. Grayson Ramírez-Yim examined and treated Jaramilla, who complained of the pain in her shoulder and head where she had been bitten repeatedly.

"Your opponent ripped out pieces of your scalp with the hair. It's going to hurt for a few days," Dr. Yim explained.

Back at the Center, Felícitas helped Paca and Micaela clean up the photos.

"Look at what we've become," she said in a resigned voice.

"What can we expect? We're surrounded by violence. We live with it every day," Paca replied.

"True, but the members of our Federation should recognize the structure of violence and rise above it. If this happens again, the two of them will be expelled. We mustn't give the impression that the Federation has internal conflicts. We have to remain united," Micaela said firmly.

Adela returned from the hospital before midnight, drowsy from the tranquilizer she was given. That night she slept soundly on the couch.

But the night was not over yet. In the living room, Carmen, Reina, Agueda and a few other women were having sweet bread and hot chocolate while they spoke with Dr. Yim, who had accompanied Adela back to the Center. Micaela walked in as Dr. Yim explained to Reina that she was pregnant, approximately six months pregnant. Micaela walked straight over to Reina, who was seated on the couch. She held one of her hands and wrapped her arm around her shoulder affectionately.

"Congratulations, Reina. I hope you have a healthy strong baby."

"Thank you, Micaela, but you should also congratulate Carmen, because she's pregnant too," was Reina's reply.

"Good God! Looks like our family is on the grow, ladies!" Micaela laughed.

"Congratulations!" the rest of the women cheered. The living room became a buzz of excitement as the women converged on the two expectant mothers, offering them their advice, maternity clothes, baby clothes and all sorts of paraphernalia.

As Adela slept peacefully, Jaramilla, who still winced from the pain, spent the night drinking coffee and chatting with the other women. At daybreak both women returned to their homes to get changed. Then they reappeared at the Federation to join the other women who were going to mass at the Church of Our Lady of Guadalupe.

🐞 🐞 🐞

By the eighth month of their pregnancy, two more neighborhood teenagers and an elderly couple had died. A young gangster was killed on his way home from school. He died because he was flashing his Hazard signs to a convoy of cars that drove by with shouts of "Maravilla rules!" When they drove past again, the young Hazard kid stood his ground by proudly showing his signs, but this time the Maravilla boys replied by cutting him down in a volley of gunfire.

The other death was of a sixteen-year-old girl, known throughout the barrio as La Sacred. Having spent most of her life in and out of different psychiatric wards around Los Angeles and Orange County, La Sacred was a notorious *loca*. She was visiting her cousins who were celebrating a *quinceañera* in Geraghty. It was during the reception after mass that the party was interrupted by a gang of homeboys from Jim Town. One of them respectfully asked to speak to his girlfriend, La Sacred. When she walked out into the street with him, they shot her and then opened fire on the rest of the crowd. Cars jammed with Geraghty homies sped off in hot pursuit of the invaders, but the lead car crashed into a parked truck, holding up the posse.

Old Taíta Fonseca was killed for complaining about a gang of *cholos* who were parking their lowriders in front of his house. Rigged up with the loudest speakers they could find, the *cholos* would sit there with their girlfriends, blasting the music. When the bass made everything in his house rattle and vibrate, Don Taíta went out and yelled at them to turn it down, threatening that if they didn't, he would call the police. The *cholos* just turned it up louder. Infuriated, Don Taíta got his hose and began spraying water through the window of one of the cars. The two homeboys inside got out and immediately shot him down. Old Taíta died in a puddle of water in the middle of his front lawn, where he and his wife had tended their rose garden.

She witnessed the whole thing from her wheelchair, peering out of their living room window. The two of them had lived in this four-bedroom house for over fifty years.

Mrs. Fonseca wouldn't let go of her beloved husband's cold hands. When they lifted his body up into the truck, she lost her breath, letting out a feeble and desperate cry for the man she had known her entire life. That night Micaela, Beatriz and Carmen brought her to the Center where Paca, as always, was waiting with her camera. After two days, Mrs. Fonseca realized that her husband was never going to come home, so she decided to die. She stopped eating and drinking, refusing to allow anything to enter her body. She didn't speak, cry or sleep. For exactly nine days, enough time to pray a novena, she sat motionless with her eyes open, looking out the window by day and waiting into the night for Don Taíta to come back for her.

"It won't be long now, my love" were her last words.

On the morning of the ninth day, Reina brought her a glass of milk and found her dead in front of the window, still sitting with her eyes open and the hint of a smile on her lips. In the last breaths of her life, somehow Mrs. Fonseca had risen from her bed, opened the window in the living room and sat down to watch the world outside, where she saw the trees, the garden flowers, the rose bushes and, perhaps, an old gentleman walking through the gate to come get her on that sunny morning.

Felícitas, Beatriz, Filomena, every woman from the Federation understood the bond of love between the Fonsecas. The two teachers, Mrs. Marbel and Mrs. Kochart, donated money to have the old couple buried at Calvary Cemetery. At the funeral both women confessed that they had known the couple for years, but neither of them had ever learned their names.

🐞 🐞 🐞

It was in the early morning when more than a hundred women invaded the house, searching for the Fonsecas' killer. Following the same *modus operandi* as before, the women ripped away the terrified boy's clothes and dragged him outdoors completely naked. Two of his brothers came to his defense, attacking Micaela and other women who were pinning him to the ground. But when they felt the cold blades of a hundred scissors snipping through their clothes, they backed away. The parents defended their boys, declaring that the accused would never hurt anyone.

"Please, he's a good boy," his mother cried.

The Federation women had heard this appeal enough times that, in unison, they began to sing the words on cue. They grabbed the murderer's mother by the hair and cut away her clothes. The same fate befell the father. Then Micaela, Felícitas and Jaramilla began the interrogation. Paca, with the help of Carmen and Reina, entered the house to take photos and search the property. It wasn't long before they emerged, clumsily lugging rifles, semiautomatics and gym bags filled with handguns and various boxes of ammunition.

"Now what do you need so many guns for? To fire them off at New Year's?" Micaela motioned to the women to load the confiscated weapons into a car and take them back to Federation headquarters. Then she turned to face the homeboy and his family.

"You killed Taíta Fonseca, and now you deserve whatever God decides for you. Don't think for a minute that you'll go unpunished. But before you leave, we want you to know that we loved that little old couple. They were living examples of unconditional love, everlasting love between two people. And what you are about to receive . . . you, your brothers, your parents, comes from God's love. We forgive you out of love, but hear this, you murderous piece of shit, you shall never come back to this barrio again without changing your ways. And that goes for your family, too. By tomorrow this house will be an empty shell that we will fill with new life. Your world no longer exists around here anymore."

With these words Micaela banished the Fonsecas' murderer and his family, ushering them through a gauntlet of menacing scissors. And they were never seen again.

"And tell your homeboy friends that if we see their ugly faces around here, we'll eat them alive!" one of the Federation soldiers yelled after them. Within an hour, Micaela had made good on her word. The house was left an empty wooden shell.

🐜 🐜 🐜

A short article titled "Federation of Witches and Murderers" appeared in *The Voice*, an independent Latino newspaper published out of East L.A. Though relegated to the back pages, the article caught the attention of a *Los Angeles Times* reporter, who decided to investigate the story for himself. He interviewed several people from Geraghty and Hazard, but he never spoke with Micaela or with any of the Federation women. Nonetheless, he convinced his editor to publish a piece in the *L.A. Times Magazine* about witchcraft and the Federation's ritual killings. He uncovered stories about how some of their victims had been stripped naked and mutilated, and how the Federation was stockpiling weapons to launch a women's army, a military legion of women purportedly dedicated to the pursuit of justice.

These weren't the only exaggerations. In the reporter's account of the Federation school, he described it as a breeding ground for racism and hate crimes, with a distinctly anti-American and anti-Anglo curriculum. This information was provided by a few people who lived nearby and knew about Micaela and some of the women, though they had never spoken with them. These locals didn't know the Federation women; they only knew what people were saying about them. It didn't matter to the reporter, though; he took their word as credible testimony. The article circulated through every county publication and, a day later, it reached national distribution. It wasn't long before radio and TV talk shows were covering the Federation, the women and their philosophy, all based on the hearsay from a few interviews.

In the days that followed, the phone rang so much at Federation headquarters that Micaela disconnected it. Sales reps were showing up at the door looking to sell school supplies and equipment. They were followed by lawyers offering legal advice and then by county officials who wanted to inspect the architecture and construction of the houses to verify that the new additions, like the bridge and the school room, conformed to local building codes. Three commissioners from city hall came to inform the Federation women that they had neither the permit nor the necessary certification to run their daycare business. Unlike previous visitors who waited outside, thwarted by the women's reluctance, the three commissioners were determined to enter the building by force. As the men slammed their shoulders into the door, five women came up from behind them with scissors in hand.

"You can go in, boys, but you'll have to leave your clothes behind," Carmen said with a smile, opening and closing her scissors.

"It's tradition," Beatriz quipped, "for anyone going in for the first time, we have to cut their clothes off. You emerge in your birthday suit to be reborn."

The men looked around nervously as more women bearing scissors and determined looks on their faces appeared. They made a hasty retreat, jumped into their car and sped off down the road.

The two volunteer teachers, Mrs. Marbel and Kochart, were both receiving visits from aggressive police investigators. This kept up until they insisted that either the police arrest them or leave them alone. The police responded by forcing their way into their homes on the pretext that they were suspects in a criminal investigation. They were warned against their involvement with Micaela and the *doñas,* whom the police identified as anarchists, extremists and dangerous political dissidents conspiring to destabilize government institutions by disturbing the neighborhood peace.

"Stay away from Micaela, Felícitas and Paca, and keep your distance from the school. We know it's just a cult of anti-government radicals and a gang of witches."

They employed the same tactic of intimidation against Dr. Grayson Ramírez-Yim, warning of the professional implications of his involvement with Micaela and the Federation women.

"Dr. Yim, you are jeopardizing your practice by associating with terrorists. You should know that these women have weapons. They're a dangerous religious cult. You would be well advised to cut your ties with them."

🐜 🐜 🐜

Grayson Ramírez-Yim saw for himself that the walls were adorned with rifles and handguns, and there were assorted boxes of ammunition scattered about the floor where both Reina and Carmen lay on their sides waiting, desperate for the pain of another round of contractions to subside. Reina's baby would be arriving soon. From the size of her protruding belly it looked like she could give birth any minute. She had been pacing the floors cursing the man who brought this disgrace upon her.

"If I see that fucker who did this to me, I'll kill him!" she screamed between the contractions that finally knocked her to the floor in the middle of the living room, where Paca stood with her video camera poised. Micaela, Felícitas and Carmen knelt by her side as Dr. Yim prepared her for the delivery. Less than an hour later, Reina gave birth to a boy, who came out screaming just like his mother. Carmen, who was enduring contractions of her own, was asked to cut the umbilical cord.

"What are you going to name him?" Carmen asked as she nestled the infant baby alongside the new mother's chest.

Reina looked at her baby and then at the women around her.

"Micaela?" Reina asked anxiously with sweat still glistening on her face. "What should we name my boy?"

Micaela drew nearer to caress them both.

"You can wait, you don't have to name him right away," she replied.

"Yes, I do! I'm afraid that he might die before I can even name him!" Reina insisted.

"There's no need to worry, Reina. There were no complications," Dr. Yim said reassuringly.

"Micaela, please!" Reina reiterated with an intensifying gaze.

"Benito. Name him Benito, Reina," Micaela obliged.

"Benito . . . Benito," Reina repeated to herself with her eyes now closed.

There was a gentle applause of approval from the women who had gathered, while Benito exercised his own little voice with apparent cries of hunger and happiness. A collective serenity settled in, lulling the mother and child to sleep. But then Carmen's shriek made the walls rattle.

That night Dr. Yim slept in the library, in case he was needed by either of the new mothers or their babies. He had fallen into a deep sleep, satisfied with having invested so much time and money in becoming a doctor. He had put the hundred thousand dollars in student loans out of his mind, convinced that they were trivial in comparison to the work that lay before him. What mattered now were the nascent lives of Benito and Teresa, whom he had just presented to the world. Carmen decided on Teresa for a name, remembering what she had learned in school about Santa Teresa and Mother Teresa: two heroines who made a lasting impression on her.

Meanwhile Mrs. Marble and Mrs. Kochart, who were determined to keep the Federation school running, were receiving an increasing amount of requests to accept new students. Most were kindergarten age, but there were also some thirty new students between the ages of six and twelve. The teachers demanded at least five hours per week of volunteer time from every mother who had children at their school. For her part, Beatriz recruited university students to help out. People from outside the barrio, who had come to see what all the talk was about, were so impressed that they donated money, furniture, food and anything else that they thought could be of use. The school's reputation grew, attracting the attention of other teachers and school administrators from neighboring counties who wanted to observe the miracle for themselves.

By the time Benito and Teresa reached their seventh month, the Federation had acquired the lots on each side of the *doñas'* houses, and then they purchased the next two plots of land on each side of these. Within a year, the Women's Scissor Federation had appropriated every lot along Beulah and Beulah Circle. And with the help of Rebecca Carter, the Santa Ana lawyer, they were negotiating to buy even more. The Federation was spreading out in all directions from the heart of the *doñas'* houses.

First it was one carpenter who showed up, followed the next day by five more, then two bricklayers, two plumbers, an electrician and a painter. The nice thing was that most of these professionals were women. They came to build additions, bridges and covered pedways to connect all the new construction. These women donated their valuable time and efforts. Some had to drive great distances every day, but they truly believed in the cause, sharing in the Federation's vision of offering a sanctuary for women in need of protection. Most arrived from neighboring cities in L.A., Santa Barbara and Orange counties. Others came from farther away. And yet, despite their geographic detachment, they were well organized. Someone was always on site to attend to any problems.

The Federation was running smoothly, attracting more and more students, harboring women in crisis and garnering support from wealthy donors. Rebecca Carter proved to be a devoted lawyer who knew how to protect the Federation from political groups and from constant police antagonism. The county sheriffs, the L.A. Police Department and even the F.B.I. were convinced that the Federation women were anarchists who were amassing an arsenal behind closed doors. It was their assumption that the women were being supplied by the same clandestine distributors who sold arms on the organized crime market. The authorities declared that, from a series of photos taken by federal agents, they had indisputable evidence that high-ranking Federation women were captured on film buying handguns. Shortly after this announcement the alleged trafficker was apprehended by the F.B.I.

The police continued to pursue gangsters, but were baffled as to why they rarely caught them with any weapons. Even the more notorious gangs were finding themselves unarmed, both on the streets and at home. There was a dramatic drop in murder and violent crime rates. According to Felícitas's calculations (she was in charge of cataloguing the weapons that were confiscated by the Federation), the crime rate had dropped by some thirty-five percent.

Naturally the women were pleased with the results of their efforts to eliminate neighborhood violence by disarming so many gangsters. Their goal was to stabilize the community by removing the fear factor, by allowing people to sit out on their patios again and take strolls down the street. By achieving this goal they would change the psychological and economic conditions that gave rise to the proliferation of gangs in the barrio. And with the eradication of gangs, so too were drugs disappearing from the streets. Every time the Federation took over a gangster's house they would destroy or confiscate all the drugs they found. The street value of the narcotics that they were eliminating was in the millions. With fewer drugs and guns, the barrio slowly began to awaken from its violent nightmare.

🐜 🐜 🐜

The improvements to their quality of life compelled many local residents to diligently protect Federation buildings. The neighborhood women were all very appreciative of the positive changes that were taking place. They even managed to stop a caravan of county sheriffs and F.B.I. agents who were closing in on the Federation. When a few women received a call that a conspicuous convoy was heading their way, they quickly ran out of their homes to empty buckets of nails into the street. Bewildered agents stepped out of their cars to inspect their flat tires. A heated argument with the neighborhood women ensued.

"You're getting in the way of a federal investigation. This is an obstruction of justice. Don't you know who we are?" the first-in-command said between clenched teeth.

While this was going on, one of the agents was racing up the street on foot toward the Federation headquarters. He burst through the gate and banged at the front door.

"F.B.I.! This is a federal investigation! Open up!"

Felícitas and Paca slowly made their way to the front door to receive their guest while Micaela and a few other women remained seated in the living room. Upon entering, the agent soon realized that all was calm in the building. Children were playing out in the yard while, from a backroom, you could hear the sound of a piano and children singing.

"And what can we do for you today, sir?" Micaela rose to face the F.B.I. agent.

"I have a federal search warrant. You must vacate this building at once to allow us to complete our search. You have already broken several federal laws. I strongly advise you to cooperate," he warned.

The room filled with women, who moved calmly toward the agent.

"Get back! Stop or I'll shoot!" he shouted, drawing his revolver.

But he was instantly swarmed by women who pulled at his belt, the buttons on his shirt, his shoelaces. Within minutes he found himself naked and being pushed back out the front door with the search warrant glued to his bare bottom. He rushed down the street to seek refuge among his astonished superiors who quickly guided him into the back of a car. Then all the cars drove off down Eastern Street, flat tires and all.

That night two helicopters flew overhead shining their powerful spotlights down on the Federation headquarters. Micaela received a phone call from the police department requesting permission to search the house. Micaela responded that they had committed no crimes, hadn't violated any federal laws and there was no reason why anyone should search their home.

"As a community we've decided that no municipal or federal agent will set foot across the threshold of this humanitarian Federation." Micaela hung up knowing all too well that the authorities' aggression was escalating: preparations had begun for laying siege against the Women's Scissor Federation.

🐜 🐜 🐜

Whether in the blazing yellow light of day or under the moonlight, in the city of Our Lady the Queen of Los Angeles, which graces both shorelines of the Porciúncula River, the unexpected had become an everyday occurrence. Just like in Mexico, people have become accustomed to awaiting the next spectacle. It could be the sensational murder of a movie star, or of a multimillion dollar athlete, or the death of a local resident after flying through the streets in a dramatic high-speed police chase. It could be the next forest fire that rages through the parched hillsides before jumping at the houses, sticking its burning claws into the wooden rooftops, incinerating every building in its path. It could be a heavy rainfall that soaks the ground to such saturation that the earth vomits it back up as furious torrents, flooding the plains, washing away the efforts but not the dreams of the people in its wake. It could be the next windstorm that uproots trees, rips away rooftops, knocks down power poles, shutting off traffic lights and cutting power to homes and office buildings, with downed wires setting fire to houses, while men and women in their cars cram into the bottlenecks of exodus from Southern California, frantic for their missing children or the things they've left behind. It could be the pollution belched out of industrial sectors, from military bases, from mounting dead bodies, from oil companies, from chemical factories, from cemeteries, from the pile-up of housing where individuals and whole families are packed like sardines into smaller and smaller lots. It could be the thunderous collisions of trucks and cars on the freeways where the noise is never ending, the eternal drone of civilization. It could

be the ubiquitous commercialization, the advertisements, signs
and billboards that pervade your line of sight every which way
you turn, the third eye that sees the world of feel-good desire,
the lustful sensation that conditions your mind whether dreaming or awake and drives you until the day you die. It could be
the earth beneath your feet that opens and closes at will, trying
to shake off its implacable scab and, buzzing over it all, the eye
in the sky, peering down from helicopters dispatched by the
media, the police, the authority, the security forces, and all on
account of me, Micaela sadly thought as she sat on the edge of
her bed looking out into the street. She closed her eyes and tried
to imagine a moment of hearing nothing at all, a moment of
complete silence, an unrecognizable calm.

But outside the crowds were gathering. The community
women brought their husbands and their children in public support of the Federation. They had organized a barricade to keep
out the authorities. The police, the paramilitaries and the heavily armed SWAT teams would all be held at bay. Traffic had
come to a halt in front of a barrier constructed of rocks and old
furniture, strewn with broken glass, nails and thumbtacks. The
doñas' houses, the administrative center and the very heart of
the Federation had been effectively secured.

For three days they waited. Every member was present:
Felícitas, Paca, Filomena and her daughter Renata, Yesenia and
her daughter Rocío, Beatriz, Jaramilla and her daughter
Catarina, Agueda Josefina Salcedo, Carmen and her daughter
Teresa, Reina and her son Benito, Dr. Grayson Ramírez-Yim,
the teachers Mrs. Marbel and Mrs. Kochart, and Micaela. They
all stuck together under siege by the authorities, while the rest
of the world watched the latest L.A. spectacle through the camera lens that circled relentlessly overhead. The shining lights
and the deafening noise of the helicopters were unending.
Ultra-powerful spotlights illuminated the houses as the photog-

raphers focused and readied their cameras for the prize-winning shot. The "choppers," as the reporters referred to them, hovered like enormous flies waiting for the opportune moment to suck out a money-making photo for the newspapers or video footage for the morning news.

At night helicopters dove down like birds of prey, but, instead of snatching up the people below, they bombarded them with insufferable noise. Music blasting out of loud speakers kept the entire neighborhood tossing and turning all night. By morning the choppers had disappeared, only to be replaced by a new squadron a half hour later. The children cried until, exhausted, they fell asleep, only to wake up a short while later to start screaming all over again. After three days Micaela asked that the children be taken away from the battle zone because they were soon going to suffer psychological damage. And so, on the morning of the fourth day, more than two hundred children, with their mothers, walked through the barricades out of Federation territory. They were met by a police brigade that ushered them into emergency clinic tents where Red Cross doctors attended to them. In the process, mothers were separated from their children for interrogation.

Meanwhile, Micaela persisted in demanding an explanation for the ongoing siege of the Federation.

"We haven't done anything against the law. All we've done is taken back our neighborhood. What crime is there in that? The entire community supports us. Why can't you? Please, leave us alone," she said repeatedly over the phone. "We want to speak with our lawyer, Rebecca Carter, so that she can explain to us what the hell is wrong with you," she demanded.

Two more days passed without any communication with the authorities, but there was a lot going on outside. As the military buildup intensified around the perimeter, within Federation territory, in the spaces between buildings, and out on the lawns, a thousand people waited for the drama to unfold. From every window of the house Micaela could see tents, recently constructed outhouses and women at work in makeshift community kitchens. The Latino community had invaded Geraghty to show its support.

The next day they realized that the police were denying passage across the barricades, effectively cutting off much-needed food and supplies for the thousand squatters. Micaela, Felícitas and Paca headed up a group to circulate among the crowd to attend to those in need and to determine who should be evacuated. Once again, the authorities detained anyone leaving the Federation grounds for interrogation. Rebecca Carter was allowed to pass through the blockade carrying only her purse, which she had filled with candies. Micaela was contacted by authorities in advance of her arrival. Walking through the crowd of supporters, Rebecca seriously doubted that any of them truly understood why they were there, camped out in the streets as they were. Though the vast majority of them were women, there were also a few husbands present who were committed to supporting the Federation. Rebecca convened with Micaela, the *doñas* and other Federation women to explain the authorities' position and to spell out what terms needed to be met before the police would withdraw. Almost simultaneously the women responded with a resounding "No!" They weren't about to cooperate, mainly because they hadn't done anything wrong in the first place. All they wanted was to be left alone to continue their community work.

Rebecca's every outside move was caught on film from the helicopters that continuously circled above the house. A number of the local neighbors had taken their TVs outside so that the people camped out in the street could watch the news reports for themselves. That night, Micaela stepped out into the street to make a declaration.

"We are not criminals, and we are not about to comply with the demands made by the police. There's no way we're going to hand over any of the guns that we confiscated from gangsters, because we're afraid that they'll come back. And, please, stop with the helicopters and the music. You're carelessly punishing our entire neighborhood!" Micaela concluded, yelling up at the helicopters that were filming her.

Around seven o'clock that night a sudden burst of gunfire was heard, followed by screams and an explosion near the *doñas'* house. Someone had shot at and hit one of the choppers, which came crashing down on a small wooden house, then disappeared in a ball of flames.

🐜 🐜 🐜

The authorities commenced their ascent toward the Federation buildings at dawn. The resistance they met was well-organized and surprisingly effective. The paramilitaries who advanced through the barricades were simply allowed to proceed unhindered through the mass of bodies. It was too late when they realized that the bodies were actually closing in on them, suffocating them with one big communal embrace. Once rendered helpless, the paramilitaries were disarmed and their clothes were cut away before they were escorted back down the hill.

By ten o'clock in the morning the authorities had regrouped, assembling their forces along Geraghty, Bonnie Beach and Hazard. They began another ascent, this time led by tanks armed with massive water cannons. The police followed on foot brandishing semi-automatic rifles. Slowly they made their way up Beulah Street, where the Federation supporters stood waiting for them. Just as before, the front lines opened a path to allow the paramilitaries to pass unhindered, but then the women closed in around them. After their warnings were ignored, the police opened fire with the water cannons, knocking down anyone and anything in their path.

The military convoy slowly made its way up Beulah, blasting its way through the crowd. But it was impossible to aim the cannons with any accuracy. They demolished the tents, the makeshift kitchens, the outhouses, even a few of the community's older homes, absolutely everything in the way. After three hours, they had regained control of the northern end of Bonnie Beach Street, all of Dobinson and Geraghty and the entrance to Beulah Street, where the crowds had now come together in greater concentrations, having fled to higher ground, contrary to what the military strategists had intended. In the wake of the offensive, many people were literally washed away by the gush of water. Some were separated from their children, their spouses, their elderly parents. The water had blown families apart, killing five people in the process. One victim was a ten-year-old boy whose broken body was washed up in a gutter. The cannon blast had broken his neck and blown him into a stream of debris that surged at the bottom of the street, where he lay, his eyes still open, submerged under the murky water. While Geraghty barrio residents retrieved the body, paramilitaries emerged from their tanks to get a better look at the damage. The sodden streets were strewn with tents, blankets, chairs, kitchen utensils, the wounded and the dead.

By four in the afternoon the L.A. police, the county sheriffs, paramilitaries and federal forces had established themselves at the bottom of the hill on Beulah Street. The helicopters returned to contaminate the night by flooding Federation buildings with blinding light and loud music. At the Federation headquarters they received a phone call asking the women to turn themselves in.

In the name of the Women's Scissor Federation, Micaela replied, "No. We are not criminals. We've committed no crimes. Go away and just leave us alone."

That night the police and SWAT units invaded homes along Beulah Street, announcing that people would have three hours to evacuate. Throughout Los Angeles and around the world, people watched on TV as SWAT teams forced children and the elderly out of their homes. The hostilities against the Women's Scissor Federation and their barrio neighbors were leading to serious human rights abuses.

🐜 🐜 🐜

The next day Rebecca returned to the Federation headquarters to communicate the authorities' terms and conditions for withdrawal, but she would leave with the same response that Micaela had given earlier: having committed no crime, they would never turn themselves in and the police should leave them in peace. As tensions continued to rise, more and more reporters and film crews arrived, eager to record the next move.

Micaela, Beatriz, Agueda and Rebecca remarked how they could no longer make out the contours of the nearby streets. Everything was chaos. You could not even see the asphalt; it was covered with so much debris after the tanks had blown away the Federation supporters. Later on that night, police and federal agents milled about under the lights from the houses. Then they cut the power, and all was dark.

The following morning began under a clear blue sky. It was one of those days when the neighborhood looked beautiful for its lush green trees and lawns, and the manicured flower gardens that people proudly displayed in their front yards. But today the sun beat down on what looked more like a disaster zone. Micaela asked the few remaining supporters outside to search for any stray animals left behind after the evacuation. By the end of the day, the Federation would take in five dogs, three cats, an aquarium and a few caged birds. When the authorities cut off the water, leaving the Federation headquarters with only their reserve of three containers of bottled water, they decided that it was time for the rest of the children to be sent out of harm's way. Rebecca, Mrs. Kochart and Dr. Yim would care for Renata, Rocío, Catarina, Teresa and Benito after they left the battlefield, while their mothers stood their ground, waiting out the siege. Swarmed by reporters as they were being detained by the authorities, the Federation evacuees kept their stoic silence. By nightfall the paramilitaries had completely surrounded every Federation building, but they would advance no further, knowing that the women inside were well armed. The L.A. police, the county sheriff's department and the F.B.I. had other plans to resolve the crisis.

It was late in the afternoon and, though there was a lot of movement of police cars and federal agents off in the distance, it seemed that, for the time being, the paramilitaries had backed off from the Federation buildings. Paca snuck outside to get better photos of the distant activities. She ran across the front lawn to hide in the thick bushes, but she was immediately detected from the eye in the sky. She scurried between two buildings, hopped over one fence after another and slipped into one of the vacant houses, or so she thought. Inside she encountered an older couple that had been hiding since the evacuation. Not wanting to attract attention to them, she thought it best to make a hasty exit, once it sounded like the helicopter was far enough away. By the third fence, she was on the run again, with the chopper hovering overhead, just above the trees.

"Stop! Or we'll shoot!" she heard over loudspeakers.

She rounded the corner of the Federation headquarters and made it up the front steps, where she was blasted from behind against the front door. Horror-struck, Micaela and Felícitas pulled her limp body through the doorway and into the dining room. Paca was alive, but she was bleeding profusely from a hole in the left side of her chest. They lifted her onto the table and did what they could to stop the bleeding. Every woman in the building gathered round her to pray—Filomena, Yesenia, Beatriz, Jaramilla, Adela, Agueda Josefina Salcedo, Carmen, Reina and Mrs. Marbel—while Felícitas held her tightly.

In a weak voice, Paca said, "Smile everyone, please," as she struggled with her good arm to take one more photo. She died with her camera on her chest, lying in the arms of her lifelong friend, Felícitas.

Together the women lifted her lifeless body and began to walk toward the door when the buzz of another helicopter made everyone stop and look up at the ceiling. This one sounded so close as if it was about to land on the roof. In a flash the house was penetrated by multiple burning missiles. They came through the ceiling, the walls and the windows, releasing a thick toxic gas that instantly filled the air. The women gagged and stumbled to find the door, but the missiles kept blowing up in front of them. Different parts of the house had caught fire. Moments later the women were all on the floor, burning. The flames spread from one house to the next, consuming every Federation building as the fire department waited idly for the inferno to run its course. The war was over. The L.A. police, the sheriff's department, the F.B.I. and the paramilitaries had succeeded in destroying almost the entire Geraghty barrio.

In the morning they discovered eleven cadavers scattered about the Federation headquarters. But the television news focused their stories on the five agents who had died three days earlier in the helicopter crash. Their State burial a week later received widespread coverage.

None of the bodies found in the smoldering ruins were recognizable, and none were identified officially until almost a year later, after much insistence by family members. Dr. Grayson Ramírez-Yim, Mrs. Kochart, Rebecca Carter, Renata,

Rocío and Catarina confirmed the names of the women who had remained in the building. They were interviewed on TV talkshows to share their experiences while living in the house under siege. Each one testified that there were twelve women in the house when it was incinerated.

The debate centered on the controversy of the bodies. The authorities insisted that they had only found eleven human corpses. The L.A. Police Department reported that they had their doubts that all the bodies found were female. They released this statement to the public based on the testimony of the helicopter pilot, who insisted that the individual with the camera that they had pursued was a man and not a woman. In the video footage, the individual jumping over fences and running from one yard to the next did not appear to be a woman. Dr. Yim, Mrs. Kochart, the two girls and Rebecca all identified the individual as Paca. The authorities maintained, however, that it was not a woman, and that he matched the description of a wanted criminal with connections to Cuba. They compared photos of the criminal with clips taken from the video footage. The juxtaposed images were shown on the news, and the police and F.B.I. spokesmen explained the detailed analysis of features, concluding that they were the same person: their wanted anti-American terrorist.

As the days went by, municipal and federal investigators announced more discoveries. They put on display hundreds of illegal weapons and box loads of ammunition. They also found cocaine and other illegal drugs in metal safes with a street value in the millions of dollars. In another strongbox they pulled out a comprehensive series of photographs that catalogued the entire neighborhood. According to the authorities, this confirmed that they had spied on the community in order to recruit more members and later force them into prostitution and into selling drugs. They also dug up over a million-dollars' worth of technical equipment, mostly computers and radios, which investigators presented as evidence that they were involved in organized crime, most likely in connection with revolutionary groups in Latin America. They concluded that the leader of the group was Micaela Clemencia, and that it was through drugs that she kept a hypnotic control over the women recruited into the Federation. The assumption was that Micaela and Paca were drug traffickers with ties to a Mexican cartel with plans to expand operations beyond Geraghty and Hazard. They were, according to public officials, the worst kind of criminals, because they hid under the guise of community activists when, in reality, their only goal was to get rich by poisoning the neighborhood youth with drugs. In the months that followed, the authorities announced more testimonies and published more evidence to confirm the official story to justify their use of force in their final assault against the Federation.

&&& &&& &&&

They held the wake at the Holy Church of Our Lady the Virgin of Guadalupe, where most of the departed women regularly attended mass with their families. It was an ecumenical service because two of the women, Filomena and Carmen, were evangelical. On the Friday that they held the wake, it was estimated that as many as three thousand people were in attendance. They prayed the rosary for twenty-four hours without interruption. All night long, hundreds of people stood in line to pay their respects. By dawn, the crowd had formed, waiting outside in the street. The deceased were then transported by bus to the San Benito Church in Montebello, where they held mass. Thousands of people lined the streets to watch the funeral procession, throwing flowers as it passed. That day, East L.A., Montebello, Pico Rivera and Whittier were closed to honor the martyrs of the

Women's Scissor Federation. The streets were covered with flowers and lined with entire families. Faithful supporters crammed into the church or gathered outside in the street, wiping away tears as the eleven little caskets were carried inside. After mass, they were transported along Whittier, then up Beverly to Rose Hills where they were buried at the cemetery overlooking the L.A. basin. The remains of the eleven women weren't officially identified until months after they were buried. Micaela Clemencia's body was never found.

           ⚙ ⚙ ⚙

     L.A. politicians working in partnership with federal agencies authorized disaster loans to stimulate sales of the empty lots. Within days, massive excavators and bulldozers wiped clean any sign of the ashen ruins. The rains came, bringing flowers and intensely green grass. A few months later, construction began, and the new owners planted their own flowers and trees. Life resumed and, in time, the public lost interest in the victims who had died in the massacre. Forsaken and forgotten, the devoted Federation women lie in the heights of Rose Hills, with a panoramic view of East L.A. and of the Calvary: the cemetery where they ought to have been laid to rest.

Also by Alejandro Morales

The Brick People

Hombres de ladrillo

The Rag Doll Plagues

River of Angels